Happily Ever Afterlife

Rachel Poli

Book Cover by AnhLuu from 99Designs.com

Proofread by Louise Stahl from Reedsy Marketplace

First edition, 2025

ISBN: 979-8-9931679-2-3 (Print)
ISBN: 979-8-9931679-0-9 (Ebook)

For those who haven't discovered their purpose yet.

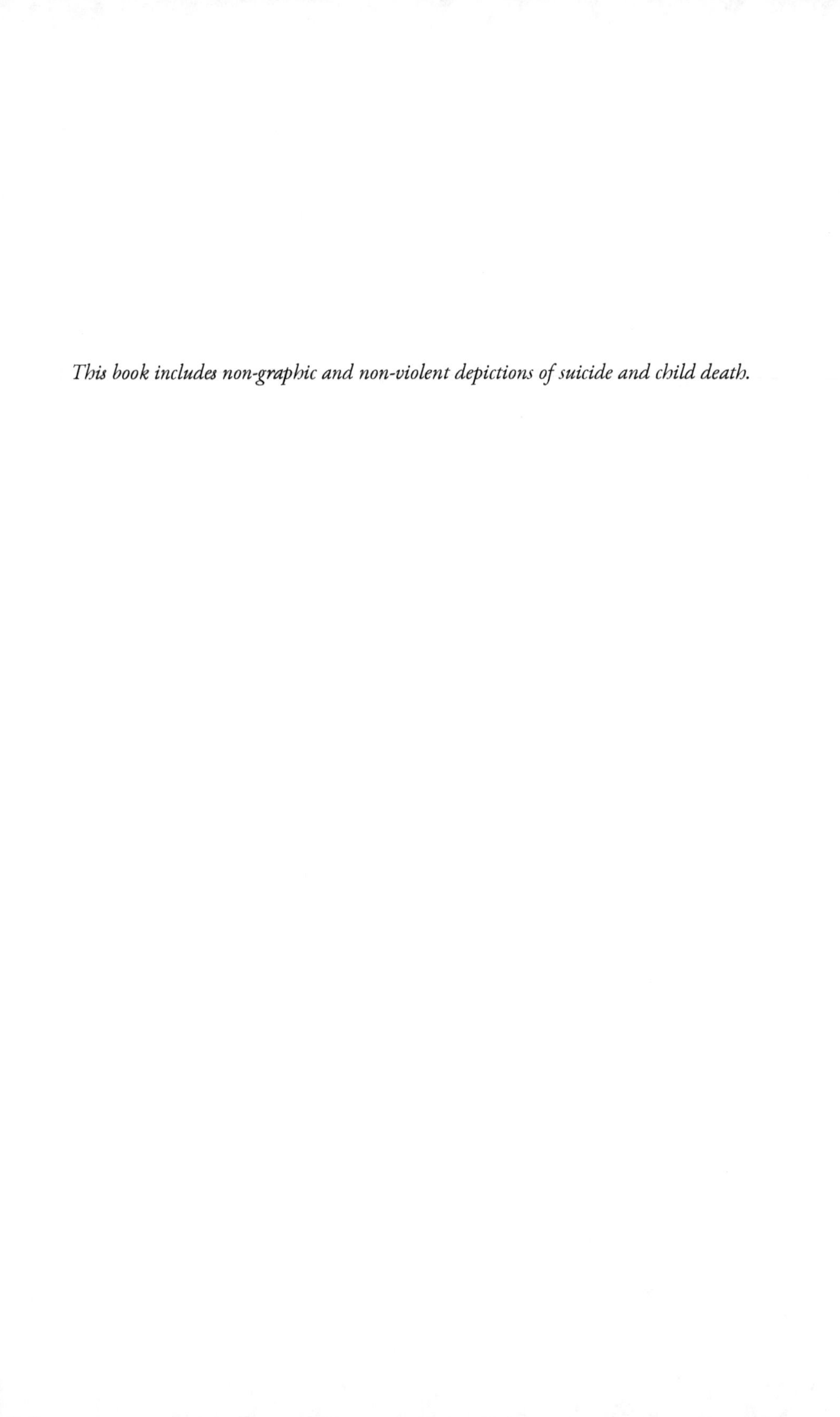

This book includes non-graphic and non-violent depictions of suicide and child death.

CONTENTS

Group One

It was difficult being in two places at once. As the Grim Reaper, I was meant to keep the Afterlife in good shape, escort newly departed souls there, but also keep an eye on the spirits already there. I was their guide. For some, their friend. Their only friend. To others, I was an enemy. I was death itself, coming to collect them too early. It was never my decision, though. If I were actually in charge, I would allow souls to have as much time in the Living World as they wished. Unfortunately, that wasn't how things worked. No matter how many times I tried explaining that, only some understood.

When someone crossed over from the Living World to the Spirit World, I was there. No one else, just me. Sometimes the souls were surrounded by friends or family. Other times, they were alone. But the moment they crossed over into my realm, they were no longer alone. They had me.

To some, this was reassuring. To others, this was scary. Rarely was I greeted with a smile. Most of the time, it was anger, sadness, confusion, a mix of all the above.

So, you can imagine my surprise when I picked up the newest resident of the Afterlife and she didn't portray any of those emotions.

I entered her house. It was old, smelling of expensive perfume and cigarette smoke. The place was unkempt, as though its caretaker had simply given up. Or maybe they could no longer keep up with it.

I never wasted time exploring the area where I needed to pick up a soul. It was best to get them quickly to bring them to the Spirit World so I could move onto the next soul that needed me. I tried not to rush, but there was only one of me and billions of them.

I poked my head into the next room, which seemed to be a study of some sort. An elderly woman sat in a rocking chair, swaying it back and forth, its wooden joints creaking at every motion. Her back was to me as she gazed out the window. Outside the window was bright, but dark clouds moved across the horizon. A storm was on its way, and I suddenly felt grateful we didn't have weather in the Afterlife.

After another moment's pause, I stepped inside the room. I remained quiet so as not to startle the woman. Sometimes, the older they were, the tougher they'd be to work with. Some were ready, others weren't. Some were bitter, and others were relieved. I didn't know how she'd be, so acting with caution was my best plan.

As I got closer, I heard her exhale a long sigh. She continued rocking, keeping a steady eye on the sky.

"I've been waiting for you."

I halted. She must have been speaking to me. No one else was here.

She looked over her shoulder, her eyes seeking me out. "You're late."

"Excuse me?" She was definitely speaking to me, though I didn't understand.

I wasn't late. Time didn't exist. It was something those in the Living World kept track of based on the positions of the sun and moon. Ultimately, though, it was human-made. Of course, she didn't know that.

She laughed, turning her attention back to the window. "Do they not have jokes in the Afterlife?"

I smirked. "Ah, so you're aware you've passed on."

"Of course."

I scanned the room, only to notice she had turned to face me again.

"My body is in my bedroom, if that's what you're looking for." She nodded her head toward a doorway to my left. "I went to bed last night and woke up like this."

I stepped closer to her. "You've had some time to come to terms with what's happened to you, then?"

She nodded. "I've been waiting for you for a long time."

I opened my mouth to respond, but she continued speaking.

"Ninety-nine is far too long for someone to be alive. I've witnessed many events in this world. Some good, some bad. I'm old. Tired. I'm ready to rest."

I remained standing in the middle of the room, unresponsive. Who was to say ninety-nine years was too long of a time? I could bet that those still living who knew and loved her would beg to differ. They'd claim they didn't have enough time with her.

Instead of correcting her, I waited patiently for her to stand. She claimed she was ready to move on, but she continued to sit. I'd let her get one last look at the sky she was about to leave behind.

Rain started falling, small droplets attaching to the window, trickling down. She held up her palm to the window, though didn't press against it.

"My husband and I used to dance in the rain. When we were much younger, of course. Now I shall never feel the cool drops of rainfall on my skin ever again." She stood, finally turning her full body toward me. I couldn't help but grin, noticing the cane that she no longer needed leaning against the wall beside her.

She stretched her arm, holding her hand toward me, and smiled. "We should go before my family arrives."

Nodding in understanding, I took her hand and our surroundings faded away.

*

The elderly woman sipped her tea, content. She sat at one end of the small round table and I sat across from her. The table was the only object in the otherwise empty, dark room. A green light illuminated the space just enough for us to make one another out. The Clock shone green to signal the session had begun.

The Crossover Room was a place in the Afterlife I met with souls who needed extra guidance. Where do they go from here? What can they do now? Is there anything they needed to talk about regarding their death? I didn't see every single spirit here—that'd be too much. Some spirits were already at peace, like this woman sitting before me. I was shocked she visited me for a session, but sometimes the souls wanted to reminisce about their past life.

The reason they joined me in the Crossover Room didn't matter. I wasn't here to judge; I was here to help guide them should they need it.

She peered into her teacup. "I'll lose my senses soon, you said?"

I nodded. "Although our spirit forms can be physical when they need to be. It takes time to figure out how to do that, but it's possible."

She sipped her tea again before changing the subject. "Does it rain here?"

I shook my head.

"Pity."

"How so?" I questioned. "Most people don't like the rain."

"Most people are fools." She smirked at me over her teacup, and I couldn't help but chuckle. I wasn't in any position to call one person a fool over another, but her words intrigued me.

She put her tea on the table, still cupping both hands around it. She leaned forward, eyeing me. "Do you remember I told you my husband and I would dance in the rain?"

I nodded.

"The first time was an accident. It was our first date. He walked me home, and a storm came out of nowhere. It poured on us. I ran for cover, trying to duck into any store that was still open. When I finally found an awning to stand under, I noticed he wasn't with me. Instead, he was a few paces behind, jumping in a puddle." She ginned at the memory.

"I called to him," she continued, "begging for him to join me. He was already soaked, and I didn't want him to get sick. He responded by reaching out and grabbing my hand. He pulled me back onto the sidewalk, under a waterfall of raindrops. His laugh was contagious. I thought him ridiculous, but how could I not enjoy the moment? No words were spoken between us. Only laughter."

I grinned at her story, waiting patiently for her to sip her tea before continuing.

"We were both sopping wet, and I was chilled to the bone. But I didn't notice it at the moment. We ran down the sidewalk, jumping in puddles. We tried catching raindrops in the palms of our hands, as if such a thing is possible. But with him, anything seemed possible." Her smile turned somber. She dipped her index finger into her steaming beverage, though I knew she wouldn't feel its liquid or heat.

She swirled her finger around the drink, anyway. "Many people don't like the rain because it gets them wet. It slows them down. It makes them tired. The rain makes the world look dull. But the truth is, there's so much beauty in the rain. It helps us thrive; it helps the planet thrive. Sure, it may tire us out, but I think that's a message from the universe telling us to slow down. To take a break, to actually see our surroundings and not look past them."

I sipped my tea, absorbed in her words. Sessions like this one were a refreshing role reversal. I was here to guide the spirits, but there were times I learned from the spirits instead.

"After all," her smile brightened once more when she brought her attention back to me. "We're meant to enjoy the journey and not the destination, right? I can't imagine how different my life would have been if we didn't dance in the rain that day. Instead of hiding, we continued our way to my house and enjoyed it. We didn't let the weather damper our time together. We chose to dance in the rain instead of waiting for the sun. Because the sun isn't always present. Life isn't always sunshine and rainbows, and if you can find someone to find the beauty in those dark times—find someone to dance in the rain with you—life will be a wonderful journey."

She took her finger out of her cup and help it up high. "That's what life is all about, isn't it?"

I clinked my cup with hers. "Life is meant to be enjoyed. I don't know what happened to you during your time in the Living World, but it seems to me you made the most of it. You enjoyed life, accepting all pieces of it."

"It's a good thing I met my husband when I was nineteen, huh? Who knows how I would have turned out." Her laughter bellowed throughout the Crossover Room.

The room glowed red. I looked toward the Clock, realizing our time was up. I hadn't noticed it turn orange, but it was obvious the soul was at peace with her passing.

Without me needing to say so, she stood up from the table, as if she knew the Clock dismissed her.

"Thank you for bringing me here and allowing me to rest," she said. The ninety-nine-year-old woman who once stood hunched over in her physical form now stood tall, steady on her feet, and beaming with confidence. She stuck out her hand, and I shook it upon standing from my chair.

"I'm going to find my husband and see what new adventures we can go on together here," she said, winking at me.

With that, she turned and walked out of the room, leaving me with one realization: I couldn't remember what it felt like to stand in the rain.

I stood in the corner of a hospital room. An adult male lay in the bed with a sightless gaze peering at the ceiling, his mouth gaped open. The machines had been turned off, so the room was still, much like the now-empty body. The only sound was of a woman quietly crying into the shoulder of the man as they stood over the deceased.

"Can they see me?"

I looked to my right, realizing the soul stood beside me. "No, sorry."

"Can they hear me?" He never took his eyes off the man and woman.

"No."

He frowned, turning away from them and looking at me. "It's just as well. I don't know what I'd say to them, anyway."

I didn't answer. No one ever knows when it's time to say goodbye. For the few who are presented with the opportunity, they never know what to say. They spend the time wishing they had more time. They're in denial. Before they know it, they've missed their chance to say what they truly wanted.

"Anyway," the soul broke me out of my thoughts, "who are you?"

"The Grim Reaper," I responded, looking down at my floor-length black cloak, gripping my scythe tighter. I thought my presence would have been obvious. The Living World made up so many rumors about me, and oddly enough, my physical features were the only things they got right.

"You finally did me in, huh?" he chuckled.

"No." I tried not to sound offended.

"It's alright," he said with a shrug. "I should thank you."

The rumor of me being death itself was wrong. No matter how many times I explained it, some spirits wouldn't understand. Of course, it wasn't something I could explain to those in the Living World.

"What do we do now?" he asked.

"I'm here to bring you to the Afterlife."

The soul nodded, as though he approved of the plan. "I never imagined this. I mean, I've often thought about death, being a sickly man and all that. If I'm honest, I never thought this is what death would be like."

I shifted my weight, not knowing how to respond. Most people didn't think this was how death went. The Living World made up many other rumors about what would happen to them when they died and they were all wrong.

"Are you ready to go?" I asked.

The spirit hesitated for a moment, but then nodded. He peeled his eyes away from the man and woman standing over his limp physical form. It looked painful for him to turn away, but he faced me, with his chest out in determination. "Let's get out of here."

*

"It doesn't surprise me I'm here. I've had one foot in the grave for years."

I sipped my tea, listening as the soul ranted about being here. They didn't seem bothered by it, but eerily relaxed.

"I didn't think I'd last as long as I did. I always had accidents, was always getting sick. In the hospital a lot. Each time I thought to myself, 'Is this it? Is this the end?' But it never was. Not until it actually was, I mean."

I nodded along. "No one knows when their time in the Living World will come to an end."

"True," he replied. "The people in my life were always happy when I'd get out of the hospital. I was too, I guess, but if I'm being honest, life was simpler in the hospital. Sure, the food sucked, and I kept being awoken in the middle of the night. The bed was uncomfortable … but it was quiet, you know?"

I didn't know, but agreed anyway. He was on a roll, so I figured I'd let him keep talking.

"I was always the first contact person for the people in my life. Family members would reach out to me about other family members. Friends would talk to me about our other friends. I kept many secrets and knew more than anyone else did. I don't know why it was me."

"They trusted you," I stated.

"Sure," he agreed. "But why? And why did *everyone* have to confide in me? I knew things about others I wasn't supposed to, always keeping a secret from someone else *for* someone else. Many secrets I am taking to my grave. That sounds like an accomplishment, but it was always uncomfortable."

"Sometimes keeping secrets isn't all that bad. It's like doing a favor for someone else," I tried to justify it, if that was even possible.

"But some of those secrets were bad," he countered. "My brother-in-law cheated on my sister."

That was unfortunate, though not the worst I'd heard.

"I never told my sister because she was cheating on him, too."

I raised a brow.

"She got pregnant from her side guy. She told her husband it was his, which caused him to panic. He was going to divorce her because he had found out he got his side chick pregnant."

The plot thickens.

"It was a mess," he groaned, rubbing his hand through his thick hair. "I never told either of them about what happened. I didn't feel like it was my place. Plus, it wasn't one-sided. They were both wrong. And yet, because they kept secrets from each other, they were avoiding the one thing that was best for them both—divorce."

"And that's what you call irony," I stated.

He let out a light laugh. "Ain't that the truth. The thing is, when they both find out the other was unfaithful to them, it'll come to light that I knew both sides of the story."

"Is that a problem?" I asked.

He gazed down at his mug, tracing the rim with a finger. "I don't know. I feel like they're going to hate me once they find out I was keeping secrets from both of them. A good brother would have sat them down together and encouraged them to talk it out. But I was too afraid to."

"I doubt they'll blame you for that. It wasn't fair of them to expect you to hold on to such heavy information."

"You're right. I know you're right, but I'm not sure they'll see it that way."

"Maybe not," I said, shrugging. "In the end, that will be on them. Not you."

"They can still blame me."

"And what could they do to you now?"

He hesitated and then smirked. "Yeah, I'm already dead. The worst they can do is defile my headstone."

"Which they won't do," I replied reassuringly. "If anything, they'll be impressed you were faithful to them both. Something they failed to do for one another."

After another moment's hesitation, the spirit tilted his head back and laughed. "Oh, *that's* irony!"

"It's true, though," I continued. "You kept heavy secrets for them and when they find out, I'm sure they'll see the irony in it, too. You respected them both, even if you didn't agree with their actions. You were a supportive brother."

He nodding along, listening to my words as he sipped his tea. "You're not wrong about that. I was going through so much with my health, and people still found a way to confide in me about their issues. I don't think they realized exactly how much I was going through myself." He looked away from his beverage and out the frame-less window, that was beside the table, into the void beyond. "It's weird because the more you're in the hospital, the more people get used to it. I think they assume, 'Oh, he's having another bad day, but he'll be back home soon.' Except, I didn't go home one day. No one visited. I died alone in my hospital room."

I frowned, knowing well enough that his sister and brother-in-law were the first to arrive as soon as they heard the news. It was probably the closest the two had been in a while. It always took a death in the family to bring everyone else closer together.

To the spirit, his sister and brother-in-law arrived after his death. All he remembered was seeing them come into the room when he was already outside his physical form. But they had arrived minutes before he moved on. The stress of the soul leaving the body had that effect. They were no longer aware of what happened around them, and the memory of their time of death was skewed because of the trauma of passing away.

It was difficult not to say anything in these moments. I wanted to tell the spirit his family did love him and were there for him. I wasn't allowed to interpret those moments for them, though. It was a memory they'd have to dig deep to remember themselves.

When I didn't answer, he kept speaking. "I'm not upset about my life, though. I still loved my family and I know they loved me. Even though I didn't get much in return from them, that's not why I did the things I did. I'm proud to have been a steady person in their lives. I'm happy they could trust me to be there for them. Or else, I don't know what would have happened."

He looked at me and smiled. "Honestly, I'm happy to be here, though. I can finally relax and take a break. It's weird knowing this is permanent. I'll never get to talk to them again or hug them. But I know I can still be there for them in some ways."

"You're absolutely right. You can head back to the Living World to visit them whenever you'd like," I explained.

"And I'll do just that," he said, standing. "But first, I'm going to find a quiet place to relax. They can deal without me for a while."

The next soul who called to me was a woman in her seventies. According to those in the Living World, that age was far too young to pass on. There was never a 'correct' age to move on, but those still alive felt that the longer you lived, the luckier you were.

Upon entering the bedroom, I witnessed the soul staring down at her body lying in bed. It looked to be asleep, not dead. I noticed the spirit smile at her former self.

I let her have a moment before making myself known. Sometimes it was best for them to not feel like they had an audience when saying their goodbyes. Yet, it seemed she had already noticed my presence. She kept casting quick glances in my direction before looking away almost immediately after. She never spoke, so neither did I.

Then she kept a steady gaze on her former self for a long time, looking it up and down, almost as if she expected it to sit up again. I knew that wouldn't happen, and I had a feeling she knew that, too.

After another moment of silence, she finally turned to look at me.

"You're getting impatient, aren't you?" she asked.

"Not at all," I replied. A little white lie never hurt anyone.

She pursed her lips into a sad smile. "I know we can't linger, but I don't want to forget my face."

I didn't completely understand what she meant, but I knew everyone grieved differently. I wasn't here to judge, and I rarely did.

"It doesn't look like me now," she said, peering down at herself again. "But I don't want to forget it."

"You don't need to worry about that," I said, reassuring her. "You can come back and visit this place whenever you want.

"Really?"

"Really."

She grinned excitedly. "Alright. We can go now."

"Are you sure?" I asked, holding out my bony hand.

Without a response, without her smile wavering, she took my hand.

*

All souls would eventually forget who they once were. It was natural and part of the process of going from the Living World to the Spirit World and then back again. It wasn't something the souls understood, nor was it something everyone in the Living World believed in. Even I didn't fully understand it, but it was the truth and something all spirits experienced.

It didn't surprise me to see this soul in the Crossover Room. She seemed to understand she had moved on, but wasn't quite at peace yet. Something bothered her—I couldn't put my finger on it, and she didn't seem to know, either.

She put her coffee mug on the table. "Sometimes people ask those hypothetical questions like what three things would you bring with you if you were stuck on an island? Or who would you rather be stuck on an island with?" she leaned forward. "I always thought those questions were silly. What are the odds of you getting stuck on an island? And, if that ever did happen, what are the odds of you being able to choose who goes with you, or have time to grab an item of your choosing?"

I shrugged. "I don't know where those questions came from, but I think they're fun for people to ponder. It's like exploring various 'what if' scenarios. Also, you can learn a lot about a person based on their answer."

She picked up her mug again, leaning back in her chair. She watched me quizzically. "How so?"

"Some people will tell you they'll grab a book. They're excited to be alone, to read in peace. They don't care where they are as long as they can have a break from the real world. Since they have a book, they'll escape to a different reality and forget they're on an island in the first place. Then you have those who will bring supplies to help them survive. Some will bring supplies to help them escape. Others will simply bring a cell phone to call for help," I explained.

She chuckled. "That is, if they have service and know the exact location of the island they're stranded on."

"True," I agreed. "There are pros and cons to every answer. You can argue the person with the book will get bored reading the same material. There's no right or wrong answer because we'll never know what would happen if you got stuck on an island with a specific item."

"And the answer would vary from person to person, even if they brought the same item," she added.

"Everyone thinks differently."

"We're all individuals."

I nodded, sipping my coffee. The spirit mirrored my movements across the table. After a moment of silence, she piped up again.

"I never understood why an island, though. Maybe it's the seclusion of it. But you'd also be secluded if you were stuck in the middle of the woods or lost in a desert. What you'd bring with you to an island probably wouldn't be the same item you'd bring with you to the desert."

"I can agree with that." I had no idea where this conversation was headed.

"I could never answer the island question," she continued. "What I would bring is a tough decision. Do I bring items to help me get off the island or things to help me survive while I find things on the island to help me escape? I'm sure I could make a raft over time. But would I survive in the open water? Probably not, but at least I'd have an answer to the island question."

I blinked at her. Her words made sense, but I still didn't understand her motives behind this conversation.

She looked around the empty room. "This is sort of like a deserted island, isn't it?"

Oh.

"Except we're not alone," she stated. "You're here, and I know other souls are here. But we don't have anything other than each other and memories of what we left behind."

"I suppose that's true," I responded.

"I think I know what I'd bring to the Afterlife with me if I was able."

I sat taller in my chair. "Oh? What would that be, if you don't mind my asking?"

"A photo album," she said softly. She took another sip of her coffee before speaking again with a sad smile. "I want to remember it all. My family, my friends, the things we did together, places we explored ... I'd like to remember the birthday parties, holidays, family reunions. Pictures help keep those memories alive. Because, over time, you simply stop thinking about those moments. When it's randomly brought up in conversation, you spend more time thinking about when the event occurred and who was there more than remembering the actual time. The conversation inevitably ends with someone dismissively waving a hand and saying, 'Ah, never mind. I can't remember.'"

She chuckled before composing herself to continue. "I know I'll forget those memories over time. That's why, if I were able to bring a photo album to the Afterlife with me ... I probably wouldn't."

I frowned in confusion. "But I thought ...?"

She looked at me, her expression still somber. "I don't exist anymore. I'm nothing but a memory now. My friends and family will grieve for me and miss me. But, as time goes on, they'll stop thinking about me every day. They'll only remember me when something happens that reminds them of me. Soon enough, they'll even forget my voice. They won't remember exactly what I looked like, only in pictures. They'll remember a version of me, but not the whole me."

Tears blinked out of her eyes. "That's why I wanted to remember my face. I know I'll forget soon. I didn't look like myself, but maybe that was because I hadn't looked at myself in the mirror for a while. I mean, *really* looked at myself. Saw me for me. Or maybe it was because my body was empty. Maybe our souls are the part of us that really shows who we are. Or maybe I remember a different version of myself, like my family and friends will remember a specific version of me. They'll remember their favorite version of me."

She kept talking before I could respond, and I let her. "That version of me might be from when I was in my twenties or forties. I liked my forties. Everyone always said your prime time would be your twenties, but not for me. I still didn't have my life figured out at that point. I barely had my life together when I was in my thirties. But it was a good life. One worth remembering."

"Even the bad memories?" I clarified.

The spirit nodded, smiling. "You can't have good without the bad."

"I agree with you there," I stated.

The Clock turned orange, which meant time was running out for this session. This soul was at peace with her passing, even though she grieved the life she left behind. It was normal, and she accepted her fate graciously.

But I had one more question before the Clock dismissed her entirely.

"You said you'd bring a photo album here, but then said you'd leave it behind. What would you actually bring?"

She let go of her mug, spreading her arms out wide. "I brought it," she exclaimed joyously.

I shook my head. "Sorry, I don't understand."

The soul giggled, standing, and then spun in slow circles as though she stood on a pedestal. "It's me."

"You," I repeated, still not getting it. Of course she brought herself. She had no choice in that.

"I can hold on to memories for as long as I can, but eventually I'll move on. When that time comes, I'll still be me, and I have everything I need to keep going."

No matter how many times I held a group session in the Crossover Room, they never got easier. I never knew if the three spirits would get along or if they'd clash. Sometimes it was difficult to get any of them to speak. Other times, one would speak enough for all of them, leaving the session incredibly one-sided. It always worked out by the end, but the beginning of these sessions never failed to stress me out.

This session included a ninety-nine-year-old woman, a middle-aged man, and a middle-aged woman. The eldest sipped her coffee contently while the man gazed around the room like he hadn't been here before. The other woman stared directly at him, though I didn't know why.

"Would anyone like to start?" I never knew how to begin these sessions.

The man jutted a thumb at the woman sitting on his right as he stared at me. "Why is she staring at me?"

"Maybe you should ask her," I encouraged, curious to know the answer myself.

Without missing a beat, he turned to the woman. "Why are you staring at me?"

She shrugged before relaxing in her chair. "Trying to figure out who you are, that's all."

"Do we know each other?"

"I don't think so."

"Then, why ...?"

"If you were stuck on a deserted island—"

Oh, here we go.

"—what would you bring with you?"

The man leaned back in his chair, folding his arms and looking upward. He didn't answer right away, but clearly thought about it.

"I'd bring my husband," the eldest spoke up.

The other lady sat taller, craning her neck to look around the man to the older woman on his other side.

"What a thoughtful answer," she exclaimed. "Bringing another person is a good idea."

The man wagged his index finger. "You know, that is a good answer. I think I'd bring someone else along, too. Then we could figure out how to get off the island together."

"Who would you bring?" the woman questioned.

"How many can come?" he remarked.

"Uh ... let's say one."

"Can it be two?"

"Why'd you bother asking if you want to bring more than one?"

The man sighed, slinking in his chair. "I don't know if I could choose between my sister or brother-in-law."

"Your sister is the obvious choice," the woman replied.

"How so?"

"She's your biological sister, yes? Your brother-in-law is related to you by marriage."

"So?"

"So, blood is thicker than water."

Shocked, the man recoiled further into his seat. "That's doesn't mean she's more important than he is."

I listened to the conversation play out for a few minutes before realizing it would end nowhere.

"Excuse me," I turned the conversation to the eldest, "why would you bring your husband?"

The man stiffened, glaring at the other woman. "See? A husband isn't related by blood."

The woman rolled her eyes at him. "That's different. She *chose* her husband. You don't choose your in-laws."

Before the man could retaliate, the elderly woman answered me. "My husband is my best friend. Why wouldn't I bring him along? He'd be great company on that island."

"But would he help you get off the island?" the other woman asked.

The elderly woman chuckled. "Who said anything about getting off the island?"

The other two spirits cast confused glances at one another before both looking at the third soul with curiosity.

"That question was always ridiculous," the eldest carried on. "Everyone interprets it as needing to get off the island, but nowhere in the question does it state *why* you're bringing these items with you to this island."

"Maybe the items are to help entertain you while you're on the island," the man added. "I wouldn't mind bringing a couple of books, or maybe even my video game system."

"Good luck charging that," the woman snickered. He glared at her.

"Listen," the eldest interrupted their quarrel, "you can bring whatever you want, but if you want company or if you want to get off the island, then bringing the people you love is your best bet. If you can bring up to three things, then bring three people. A team of four is better than one. You can use the strengths of others in areas you might lack. If your goal is to escape the island, then when you get on that raft, you can take turns paddling. Everyone chips in and everyone can rest."

She had stunned everyone in the room, including me. I didn't think she'd be the type of person to have thought of that question so seriously. She had either thought about it before or she really was that good at thinking on her feet.

"If I could bring up to three people, then I'd definitely bring my sister and brother-in-law. Their side partners wouldn't be there, so many things would go back to normal," the man stated. Then, he sighed, shaking his head. "Or maybe they'd argue the whole time."

The other woman patted him on the shoulder. I assumed it was meant to be reassuring, but she had no idea what he was talking about. She changed the attention to herself. "I don't know who I'd bring."

"It was your question and you don't have an answer?" the man asked.

She shrugged. "I never thought about *who* I'd bring, only *what*. If I need someone to help me get off the island, then I'd need to really think about who'd be best for the task."

I held up a hand to silence them. Two of the spirits turned their attention to me while the eldest hummed to herself while sipping her beverage.

"We've established the question never specifies why you need the items or companions. It also never suggests any sort of goal. The assumption is that you need to get off the island, but what if you were there permanently? What if the island was your new home and you're starting from scratch? Would your answers change?"

"No," the elderly woman replied, undoubtedly. "My husband and I would have another shot to spend the rest of our lives together. It'd be amazing to have the chance to do that again."

I grinned at her response before turning to the other spirits.

Quietly, the woman spoke up. "I said to you before I wouldn't bring the photo album. But if I had no way of getting back home, then yes. I'd bring the photo album. I'd want to remember my old life, the people and places I loved once upon a time."

"Wouldn't that make you sad?" the man asked.

"Absolutely," she said, nodding. "That doesn't mean I'd want to forget those memories."

He slouched in his chair, crossing his arms and legs.

"Something the matter?" I pressed.

He shrugged. "I don't think I'd want to start a brand-new life with my sister and brother-in-law, despite how much I love them. If I brought something sentimental like a photo album, I know I'd regret not asking them to join me. I think I'd want to bring something from home that made me happy, that helped me to relax. I'm tired and stressed from my time in the Living World. I just want to rest."

Before I could answer, the elderly woman replied, "That's a respectable answer, too. Don't think of the island as something you're stuck on. Think of it as an oasis." She cast a sly grin my way. "We're already here, in the Afterlife. Our oasis. It's a time for us to recharge and reset."

"Reset?" he echoed.

She sipped her coffee without responding, a grin still formed across her lips. I too grinned, realizing she understood more than she let on. She knew she'd find her way back to the Living World soon enough. They all would.

The Clock turned orange as the other woman spoke. "I didn't want to forget what I looked like. I didn't want to forget what my home looked like. But now that I'm here, I feel like we're on a deserted island. We didn't get the chance to bring anything or anyone with us. If we view the Afterlife like an oasis, we'll soon realize we don't need anything or anyone else. We only need ourselves, though that's not to say we should forget about everything else."

"Of course not," the man added. "I could never forget my sister and brother-in-law, even though I don't want to be part of their drama anymore. No more secrets, no more going behind someone's back. I want my oasis to be calm. I think that's something I need for myself. Does that make sense?"

I nodded. "It sometimes gets to a point where you do so much for others that you forget to do things for yourself along the way."

The middle-aged woman grinned. "I liked reworking the question. Our goal isn't to escape to where we came from, but to adapt to this new living style. It's the only way we'll grow."

With agreement from the other souls, the Clock turned red. We said our goodbyes, and I watched them vanish as they floated farther away and out of the room.

Their conversation gave me pause as I thought about how the Afterlife could be an oasis for me. I couldn't remember what it felt like to dance in the rain. I didn't have skin. I couldn't scratch an itch. Feel a bruise. Caress a loved one.

I couldn't remember any past lives I've lived—if I ever lived any at all. I had nothing to bring with me to this island. An island I don't think I'm ever meant to leave.

GROUP TWO

"PLEASE, WAIT."

Another hospital visit. Most people enter with the expectation they'll find what's wrong, get a cure, and go home. This soul went into surgery under the assumption she'd wake up feeling better. Instead, she woke up to me.

When she asked me to wait, she wasn't pleading for an extension. She knew when she awoke standing over her body, lying still on the operating table. She watched the surgeon and nurses scurry around the room—some in a panic, some succumbed to their patient's fate.

I knew this spirit's internal clock had reached zero. It didn't matter how good these doctors were. Her time was up. To me, she didn't seem upset. Dejected, but not upset. Almost as though she had expected this outcome. It's only a shame she couldn't be surrounded by her loved ones when it happened.

So, we waited. We watched in silence as the medical staff shut down the monitors and machines. We waited—for what seemed like forever—in agony, as the surgeon exited the room to announce the death to the family. We followed as the staff moved the body to a quieter, smaller room, where we waited some more as the remaining medical staff made the body look as decent as possible.

Then, as if in slow motion, the family entered the room.

"That's my daughter," the spirit said to me as a young woman crossed the room. "Her daughter. My son and his wife and daughter. My husband is the one standing beside my youngest daughter." She heaved a long sigh. "I wonder what they're thinking about right now. Do they regret encouraging me to go through with the surgery? Do they think they're at fault? Their hope of having more time with me has been completely shattered by an abrupt end."

I didn't have words of comfort for her. Sometimes it was best just to listen.

We watched her family hug one another, crying over her lifeless body, kissing her forehead, or simply holding her hand. Soon, the wailing died down and a heavy weight blanketed the room. The family tried gathering their bearings, only some being successful.

"I don't wish my family to waste their precious tears on me."

I looked to my right to see the spirit smiling through her own tears.

"I'm sure they know how much I loved them. How much they all meant to me. Or else I wouldn't have tried the surgery. I think, keep down, they knew this would be the last they'd ever see of me." She looked at me, her grin unwavering, but her eyes told another story. "That's the hardest part of it, isn't it? Most of the time, you don't know when it'll be the last. You don't know when it'll be over. Even if you did know, you'd push those thoughts away. You'd stay in denial because then maybe it won't come true." She looked at her family again. "You'll see them again. Talk to them. Laugh with them. Create one more memory to hold on to."

*

"This is it, huh?" the soul spoke with her arms crossed. She wandered the Crossover Room, throwing her gaze around.

"This is it," I replied, stretching my arms out to showcase the nothingness around us. "Would you like to sit?" I pointed to the chair across from me at the table.

She paused her pacing to look at the empty seat. "What happens if I sit?"

"You'll be at the table with me and we'll talk." I never had anyone question a chair before.

She let out a relieved sigh before chuckling. "Sorry, I thought this would transport me somewhere." She sauntered over to the table and sat down, leaning back to make herself comfortable.

"To where?" I couldn't help but smirk at the thought.

She shrugged. "Back to the real world, I guess?"

The real world, huh? It was interesting to me she thought the Spirit World was less 'real' than the Living World. Yet, it made sense. For these souls, the Living World was where they had a family, made friends, created memories. They lived. The Afterlife was dull, and while the spirits could easily make connections with one another here, it certainly wasn't the same as being alive.

Souls were well accustomed to the Spirit World, though they'd forget about it the longer they're in the Living World. This spirit would indeed find her way back to the Living World again, as they all did. It just wouldn't be the same as they remembered it now.

"Care for a drink?" I offered, changing the subject.

She nodded.

"Coffee? Tea? Hot chocolate?"

"Coffee," she replied, her tone skeptical.

I made two coffee cups appear before us, both piping hot.

She grinned, picking up hers. She breathed in its rich hazelnut scent. "Who knew the Afterlife had coffee, of all things?"

"The Afterlife can have whatever you need, within certain limits," I stated.

The soul took a sip before gently placing the mug on the table. She stared into the cup as though she saw something in it. "I had to fast before my surgery. I couldn't eat or drink anything past six the night before. That meant my final cup of coffee was over twenty-four hours prior to my operation."

She took another sip. "It was tough not having a coffee before heading to the hospital. Deep down, I knew I would never have another cup of coffee again. I would never step foot inside my home again. The home my husband and I bought together when we were married. The home that helped us create a family, build a life together."

I nodded along, not wanting to interrupt.

"My oldest daughter lives away at college and my son lives with his wife and my granddaughter. So, the only people I saw before surgery were my youngest and husband. I knew I'd never see them again, or even speak to them. Hug them, kiss them." A tear rolled down her cheek, and she chuckled, wiping it away with the back of her hand. "You usually don't know when something will be the last, but this time I knew. I saw it coming because of all the other times I missed as the last time."

"Care to explain?" I prompted.

"Take my children, for example," she began, sitting forward. "I used to rock my youngest to sleep whenever she was sick. You don't notice it at first, but as she got older, she didn't need me to rock her anymore. She was too big to sit on the chair with me, anyway. There was a time I rocked her to sleep for the last time, and at the moment, I didn't realize it. Then, my oldest daughter had the hardest time sleeping as a kid. She was afraid of the dark, whatever was under the bed, in the closet, the clock ticked too loudly, you name it. She slept in bed with my husband and me for years. The older she got, the more I prayed she'd get a good night's sleep in her own bed so my husband and I could finally get a solid night's sleep. Then, one night, when she was almost six-years-old, she put herself to bed. That was that. The previous night was the last she'd ever cuddle close to me, and I didn't know it. Instead, I wished it away. My son and I used to play pretend with his stuffed animals. Then one day, we just didn't. And we never did again."

She gazed into her mug as though she were about to sip again, but she looked at me once more. "My children and I would play outside all the time. We'd ride bikes, go for nature walks, draw with chalk ... but then, somewhere along the way, they'd spend most of the afternoon doing homework. Or they'd have a sports practice to attend, hang out with their friends. There came a day when I would never draw with chalk again with my kids and I didn't realize it."

Together, we sipped our drinks. I had a feeling she wasn't finished getting her thoughts out of her head, so I silently willed her to continue, and she did.

"I had a roommate in college. We got through all four years together. On the last day, we hugged goodbye and swore to keep in touch. I got married, and she got a job out of state. Little did we know that 'see you later' would last forever. My husband got laid off from his job and they didn't tell him until the morning before his shift. The previous day was his last day at work, his last time seeing his co-workers, and he didn't know it."

She opened her mouth to continue, but then laughed, as though embarrassed she spoke too much. "I think you get my point. When you're alive, you take things day by day but never know if what you do, who you speak to, or where you go will be the last time."

"I understand," I agreed. "Many beings in the Living World take those moments for granted. If you want to keep in touch with someone, you have to make it happen. Everyone gets busy, they all live their own lives, and if you want to be part of someone's life, then you have to make that effort."

"I agree," she murmured. "As for the children, they simply grow up. There's no stopping those moments from going away, it's part of life. It's a good thing, but ... it still hurts. I miss those days."

"It's normal to miss those days. Missing those moments means you've made memories."

She smiled. "But it's still so weird to think about, you know? I don't even remember the last day I drew with chalk with the kids. I certainly didn't know the next day would be raining. Then the kids would have a sports game. Then a play date. Then it'd be a raining again. During all that time, the chalk sits in the hallway closet waiting to be remembered. But it only gets remembered when you clean out that closet a year later and think to yourself, 'Wow, we haven't used this in a long time. Why do we still have it?' Then you donate it. But that's the nail in the coffin, isn't it? Once you get rid of the chalk, you're only left with its memory."

The Clock turned orange, and I realized this soul was moving on. It wasn't due to anything I said. She figured it out on her own, though I believed she began that process before she laid down on that operating table.

"Thanks for that," she said, with no sign of any tears. "I needed it."

"That's what I'm here for," I replied, as the Clock turned red.

As I watched her vanish from view, I felt her pain. It's true you never know when something will be the last. It's what made living scary and exciting at the same time. It's how you handle those situations, how you chase what you want.

The problem is that most people don't know what they want until it's too late.

I stood to the side of the road, looking onward to where a young woman lingered over her physical form in the middle of the street. Those still in the Living World gathered around—some in the street, others on the sidewalk. They all gaped in shock at the hit-and-run that occurred before their eyes. The death was instant, and instead of watching the spirit detach itself from its physical form, I watched the SUV skid around the corner, fleeing the scene.

"Get up."

I turned away once the vehicle was out of sight, eyeing the spirit who glared at her body.

"What are you doing?" she demanded at it, her hands balled into tight fists. "Get up!"

Did she know she was dead? Or was she in denial? It was hard to tell, especially since I didn't think she noticed my presence at all.

She attempted to nudge the body with her foot, but it passed through.

I stepped off the curb, preparing for the worst. I didn't expect her to come with me quietly and I needed to handle this crossover delicately. Before I could get much closer to her, the crowd swarmed the body. The spirit staggered back, clutching where her heart would be.

"Is she dead?"

"She must be. No one could have survived that."

"Her body went flying!"

"Did anyone call the police?"

"What about the car? Anyone get a license plate?"

The spirit stepped toward another woman. "Excuse me." She tapped the woman on the shoulder, but like her foot, her hand went through the lady's shoulder. She gasped, staring at her hand as though it weren't real. "No, no, no!"

"Hello?" I called out of her, walking closer, though I don't think she heard me.

"I'm not dead. I'm promise, I'm not dead!" she called out into the crowd.

"Should we check for a pulse?"

"Yes, please!"

"Nah, she's definitely gone."

"No! I'm right here!" the woman screamed. She darted toward the man, who dismissed the suggestion. She swung her fist at his head so hard, her entire self fell through him. I watched as she stumbled to keep her footing and he shivered, but otherwise, seemed unbothered.

I stood behind her, gently placing a hand on her shoulder. "Excuse me."

She turned her head around so fast I could see the relief in her eyes. She must have thought I was alive and could see her. Oops.

Her grin faded as she looked me up and down. Then it clicked who I was and realization sunk in. She rolled her shoulder, shaking my hand off her, glaring at me. "Absolutely not!" She ran over to the closest person who stood over her dead body.

"Splash some water on my face! I'm dreaming!" she shouted in the person's ear, though they didn't flinch.

"You're not dreaming," I calmly said, holding my hands up to show I meant well.

She twisted her body around to face me. Her anxious expression turned to a dark glare. She pointed at me as though I were a monster. "I'm not listening to you! You stay away!"

I obeyed, dropping my arms back to my sides. Denial was always a rough stage and tricky for me to navigate, depending on the spirit's emotions. On one hand, her denial ran so deep it was best for me to get her to the Afterlife as soon as possible. Yet, she was in such a fragile state, I had to tread carefully or else she'd break completely.

"The police are on the way."

"Poor thing ... I hope they find the driver who did this."

"What a weird way to go."

"Such a shame."

Hearing the crowd talk over one another, the spirit spun in circles, her eyes wild and desperate to spot anyone who could see her—anyone who wasn't me.

"How did it happen?"

"People always drive too fast on this road."

"Yeah, but she was jaywalking."

"It's crazy how small mistakes can have such dire consequences."

I narrowed my eyes at the crowd. None of this helped, not that they were aware the woman's spirit still lingered. She dropped to her knees, clutching her head in her hands. The crowd kept talking over one another about the things she should have done to avoid being hit, while others defended her and blamed the driver.

"Freak accidents happen."

"She was in the wrong place at the wrong time."

Some souls wouldn't mind this environment. They'd be too much in shock to comprehend what was happening. But this spirit heard every word, completely aware of what happened, powerless to change it, too distraught to accept it.

She remained on the ground, gently cradling herself with shaking shoulders as she cried and muttered to herself. "I didn't do anything wrong ... it's not my fault ... I'm not dead ... I'm here ..."

I walked closer to her, weaving through the crowd despite being able to go through them. I kneeled in front of her, keeping my hands off so as not to spook her again.

"I'm sorry this happened to you," I quietly spoke. "I'm here to help, to bring you some place quieter. More private. But we need to leave now."

She peered at me through her fingers. Her eyes were bloodshot and wide, as though silently pleading with me to either bring her back or make this all go away. I wasn't sure which.

I heard sirens in the distance as someone in the crowd shouted, *"Good! The police are almost here!"*

I didn't want her to see or hear any more than she already had. I held out my hand. "Please," I urged.

Her gaze lingered on my bony fingers a few beats. As if in a trance, she finally gave in and placed the palm of her hand in mine.

*

"I thought you meant you'd make everything go away."

I sipped my coffee, sitting at the round table. Technically, I did make everything go away. Just not in the way she had wanted. I listened to her complain, allowing her to get whatever she needed to off her chest.

A cup of tea sat opposite me on the table, but the spirit hadn't touched it. She didn't sit at the table, but stood beside it, gazing out the window.

I often wondered what the spirits saw out that window, if anything at all. In truth, I didn't know why the window was put there, but some souls seemed to appreciate its presence. Maybe it made the Crossover Room feel more homey, but gazing into an abyss didn't scream "home" to me.

"You couldn't bring me back?" she asked, looking at me with a casual glance over her shoulder.

"No," I replied bluntly.

"Why not?"

"Your time was up."

"But—"

"I said what I needed to get you back home. I apologize if that felt like a lie."

"Home?" she echoed, turning her whole self to face me now. She crossed her arms, staring quizzically at me. "This is not my home."

"It is," I said with a dip of my head. "You're back in your spirit form, which makes the Afterlife your home."

"*Back* in my spirit form?" she mimicked again.

I nodded once more. It was a process I wasn't inclined to explain. The souls would figure it out on their own in due time. Luckily, she didn't inquire further about it.

Instead, she hoisted her hands on her hips. "What did I do to deserve an early death? I thought I was a good person."

I shrugged. "No one deserves death. Then again, no one deserves to live, either."

In one fluid motion, she sat down in the chair opposite me, never once taking her intrigued gaze off me. "What a weird thing to say to someone."

"The definition of good varies with every individual. Being good or bad has nothing to do with death. If you believe you were good, if you made choices in your life that came from your heart, then sure, you were good."

The spirit shook her head in disbelief. "Then, why did I die so young?"

"You're not the youngest to have arrived in the Spirit World," I said, knowing that would be of no comfort to her, but it was the truth. She wasn't the youngest, nor the oldest. She wasn't the first one to arrive here for a seemingly unexpected death, or a freak accident, and she certainly wouldn't be the last. "Even I don't know why some come to the Afterlife from a disease versus an accident versus something else."

She thought for a moment before a chuckle escaped her lips. "But you're the Grim Reaper. Shouldn't you know?"

I stiffened. "Who I am doesn't mean I have all the answers. My identity has nothing to do with the way the universe works."

She furrowed her brows at my statement.

"Your time was up," I said simply. "Your internal clock reached zero, and it was time for your soul to leave its physical form."

She nodded ever so slightly before allowing herself to laugh. The spirit turned her head to the window once more, shaking her head in disappointment, yet still wearing a smile. "So, my decision to ignore the crosswalk signal wasn't an accident. I made that choice because my time was up and my spirit needed to get out of my body. It was an unconscious decision."

I sipped my drink, letting her speak.

"I don't even remember thinking about it. Maybe I pushed the button for the crosswalk, but I didn't wait. I saw it was clear to cross at that moment and stepped off the curb. I walked because an unknown force willed me to in that moment."

I hummed. It was a roundabout explanation, but she wasn't wrong. Sometimes I wondered if the internal clock ticked down to something specific, something that would call the spirit back to the Afterlife. It never occurred to me that maybe it counted down to nothing. That when it reached zero, whatever was around the spirit would be their undoing. Some people in the Living World believed in fate and destiny. Maybe that had more of a pull in the way the universe worked, more than even I knew.

The spirit sighed, breaking me out of my thoughts. "Why did it end so abruptly?"

I didn't have an answer for that.

"Earlier, you said no one deserves death or life." She looked me in the eye. "What did you mean by that? Are we all pawns?"

"Pawns?"

"From the universe. Does the universe just … play with our lives?" she pressed on in an eerie tone, one that made me believe she wasn't sure what she asked.

"I wouldn't say that." I didn't know how else to respond.

"Then, please explain," she continued. "I'm trying to understand."

I'm trying to understand, too.

I placed my coffee cup on the table, relaxing my shoulders. "I'm afraid whatever I tell you won't provide any comfort."

She leaned forward, resting her elbows on the table with her hands folded. "I'm not looking for comfort. I'm looking for the truth."

Could I give her the truth? Did I know the truth? Why were the living and the dead separated as they were? Why did any of us exist at all? I've been presented with such questions before, usually by spirits attempting to move on. The only answer I was able to give was this.

"If we knew the truth, if we knew all the answers, then there'd be no point in living."

"But I'm dead now," she said flatly.

I smirked. "Just because you're dead doesn't mean you stop living."

She hesitated for a moment, but eventually relaxed. She chuckled again. "Alright, fine. Keep it a secret."

The Clock turned orange, though the session didn't feel like it neared its end.

"I keep no secrets," I defended myself. "You wanted the truth, and that is the truth. Maybe we're not meant to know."

The soul stood and the Clock immediately turned red, almost as though she dismissed herself.

"You must know something," she said, staring at me with an amused expression. "Or else, why would you be in this position?"

I scoured my mind for the right response, but nothing presented itself.

"You can't be the Grim Reaper without knowing all the answers. Without knowing the truth."

She discharged herself in a friendly manner and exited the Crossover Room without allowing me any time to respond.

I stared at the blue rose sitting in the center of the table. The rose that I made when another spirit wanted to decorate. Why was that something only I could do?

Its blue coloring glistened against the darkness of the rest of the room, a color not typically found in the Afterlife. It made me wonder.

If we were all living in some form, why were we worlds apart? And why, of all the spirits who crossed over, was I the only Grim Reaper when I was equally left in the dark?

"I didn't get the chance to finish anything I should have."

"I'm sure you accomplished some things."

"No, I don't think so."

The next soul and I stood in the back of a hospital room, conversing as we watched the family surround her corpse. Some cried, others sat in silence. Others swapped stories about the spirit when she was alive. It felt like a funeral, even though she had moved on only moments ago.

"What makes you think that?" I continued.

She shrugged. "I had dreams. But there were things I needed to do, so I never got the chance to do what I wanted."

"Like what?"

"Find love. Start a family. Get a good job."

"Those were your dreams?"

"No," she replied, shaking her head.

"But you mentioned dreams," I pressed.

"But I had to do what I needed first." She dismissively waved her hand. "Not that it matters. I can't do anything now. I'm dead."

I didn't respond, figuring this conversation would be best suited for the Crossover Room.

When I arrived here, she was already waiting for me. She understood she was dead. She watched her loved ones grieve for her, but didn't seem to grieve for herself or for them. Although, judging by her words, I'd guess she felt regret more than anything else.

She had been sick on and off. I suspected she thought her time neared its end, leaving her unsurprised when she awoke outside her physical form. She greeted me as though we had met before. Maybe we had in another life.

We stood in silence for quite a while, watching the scene unfold before us. More family and friends entered the room, taking turns mourning the body. Once in a while, a nurse poked their head in. After the third time the nurse entered the room, the spirit turned to me.

"Shall we go?"

"Are you ready?" I asked, glancing at her.

"No," she answered quickly. "But I don't have much of a choice now, do I?"

I remained quiet. She wasn't wrong, but if she wanted more time to linger, I could give it to her.

Instead, she shook her head as though shaking certain thoughts away. "Yes, let's go. There's no sense in dilly-dallying."

*

It didn't take long for the spirit to arrive in the Crossover Room. She requested coffee, so I made coffee appear for me, too. She sat down at the table, making herself comfortable, and the Clock turned green, starting the session. Immediately, she spoke.

"Did I run out of time because I didn't do what I was supposed to?"

It wasn't often I'd come across a soul who thought death was a punishment for not living their life a certain way. "How were you supposed to live your life?"

"Marriage, kids. You know."

"I don't know."

"How do you not know?" she seemed taken aback, but I shrugged.

"There isn't one specific way to live," I stated. "You live it how you want to. Go after those dreams you said you had."

"Dreaming doesn't get you far," she quipped.

"How so?"

"You're the Grim Reaper, right?"

"Correct."

"Why don't you know anything?"

That was rude.

"What am I supposed to know?" I said, feeling utterly stupid.

"Everyone is supposed to live their life a certain way," she repeated. "We learn things as children, from academics to social skills, emotional balance, whatever. We grow older, go back to school to get a degree, earn a job that pays the bills. You following me? Then, we're supposed to find a life partner, build a home together, have children. Rinse and repeat. The circle of life."

I defined it as a life cycle, not a circle, but everyone had their opinion.

"Is that how you wanted to live?" I asked.

She sat taller, looking annoyed. "That's what I was *supposed* to do."

"Says who?"

"Everyone."

"Everyone lied to you then." I sipped my beverage.

Her mouth gaped in a silent gasp. "Isn't that why we're put on earth? To keep it turning?"

Humans didn't physically push the earth toward its orbit, but sure. "I don't think you understand what I'm trying to say."

Grumpily, she crossed her arms. "You're not understanding what I'm saying."

I ignored her. "You live your life as *you* want to. There are times when you'll need to do things you *have* to, but overall, your life is yours. Do what you want, what makes you happy. Make the right choices for you and your loved ones. If that includes getting married and having children, then great. If not, that's equally great."

"But—"

"Did you *want* to get married and have children?"

She thought about it. "Well, it would have been nice to find someone to grow old with. Not that it matters since I didn't get a chance to grow old ..." her voice tapered off before speaking up again. "But that's why I'm asking if I died early, because I didn't start that process yet."

This was going to be a long session.

"Death isn't a punishment."

Her gaze scanned the room before settling it back on me. She winced at what she was about to say. "It kind of looks like one," she muttered, then pointed to the blue rose. "Even the decor is bleak."

I narrowed my eyes, slightly offended. "Hey, I created that."

She pressed her lips into a sorry smile. "It's impressive you created such a realistic-looking flower, despite its unrealistic coloring."

"It is real."

She ran her fingers through its petals, phasing through it. "It's a hologram."

"A what?"

"It doesn't even smell."

"Because you're losing your senses."

"Huh?"

"Never mind," I groaned, pinching the bridge of my nose. "Listen, you're here because your time was up in the Living World. Your internal clock reached zero. Everyone has a certain amount of time there, though no one knows how much. That's why you live as you want."

"How was I supposed to know that?" she countered.

"That's the point. You can't waste time worrying about what others are doing or what you *think* you should be doing. Life isn't a race."

She frowned, slouching in her chair. "But I just wanted people to be proud of me ..."

"I'm sure they already were proud of you."

"I didn't contribute anything to the world, though. I couldn't even keep the family name going." Her gaze wandered to the ground, sadness flooding her eyes.

"You didn't want any of that, right?" I asked delicately.

She shook her head slowly before snickering. "I wanted to be an astronaut. I didn't pursue it though because I knew you can't meet the love of your life in space. At family reunions, I'd always get asked where my boyfriend was. Why wasn't I married? My biological clock is ticking ... or whatever. All my friends got married one by one. Before I knew it, I was the third wheel. I was so behind and no matter how hard I tried to catch up, I just couldn't." She looked up at the ceiling, blinking tears from her eyes.

I frowned, feeling for her. I understood the pressure she felt most of her time in the Living World. She wasn't the only one. Society expected too much of its inhabitants. The problem was, society was the inhabitants. It was an issue everyone chipped in to create.

"Doing what you want is what brings real happiness," I began. "Most people get upset or jealous when they see someone else has made it to the finish line. But everyone has their own finish line. We're not all aiming for the same goals. At least, we shouldn't be, or else the world would be an extremely dull place."

Her eyes blinked toward me, but her chin still tilted up.

I continued. "When someone crossed their finish line, that's good. They found what success means to them and they're happy. And good for them, because that was a difficult thing for them to do. They walked a long path. Sometimes they ran, other times they crawled. They'd take a wrong turn now and then, sometimes needed to stop and rest. But they'd always find themselves back on their path. You've done the same on *your* path."

She leveled her head to face me directly, focusing on my words.

"Your path doesn't look like theirs," I explained. "You can follow in someone's footsteps, but only so far. At some point, you'll come across a fork in the road and decide which path is best for you. Sometimes it'll be similar to someone who's already walked that part of the road, but most of the time it's different because you're an individual. You're unique. Only one path is meant for you and only you. So, which path do you want? Which one will make you the happiness?"

The spirit continued to stare at me, her eyes wide with curiosity. When she didn't speak, I continued my speech.

"It won't be easy. It never is. One day you'll take a leisurely stroll down the path, other days you might run. Sometimes you'll need to crawl or stop for a bit. Wrong turns will occur whether you like it or not, but that doesn't mean you won't find your way back. Only you will find the courage and determination to find your way again." I grinned, looking her in the eyes. "And when you make it to your finish line, you'll be proud of how far you've traveled. Amazed at what you accomplished. Some people will feel jealous, but only because they haven't crossed their finish line yet. That's all part of it. You can't compare the length of time it takes one person to make it while you're still walking. After all, you haven't completed the path yet, so how could you possibly know how long it'll take? As long as you're still walking, you're in good shape. You'll get there."

There a moment of silence before the spirit picked up her coffee. "Damn," her voice echoed into the mug as she took a sip.

"You didn't walk on the wrong path. You unknowingly walked the route that was right for you. The path you wanted, and that's a good thing," I concluded.

"You're right," she muttered, though a smile formed on her face. "I did accomplish a lot, and even though things were tough, I wouldn't change anything about the way I lived. I might have been the third wheel around my friends, but I was still happy for them."

"Were they the ones at the hospital?" I asked.

"They were."

"They must have been proud of you."

She laughed, wiping away a tear. "I suppose so. I wasn't on the same level as their lives were, but I guess that didn't mean they loved me less. I certainly didn't love them any less." She frowned once more. "I still don't understand what the point of my life was. I'm pretty sure I didn't reach my finish line before dying."

I shrugged. "Maybe that's something you'll have to figure out visiting the Living World."

"What do you mean?"

"Go back and check in on your loved ones."

"Would that do any good?"

"If it's something that would make you feel better, then yes."

She thought for a moment. "I think it'll make me sad. Like I'm missing out on something."

"You won't know unless you check it out." I held up my hands. "But only when you're ready. There's no rush."

We sat in silence the rest of the session. Her gaze wandered the room before settling on the vacant window. She stood, peering through it, lost in thought. I sipped my coffee, giving her the space and time she needed.

But she was never ready to talk again. Soon enough, the Clock turned red. She thanked me for my time as I dismissed her. As she left, I made our cups disappear.

She hadn't realized it yet, but she did cross her finish line. It just didn't look the way she expected it to.

Three ladies shared the table with me, chatting amongst themselves. Neither of them brought up their deaths. They spoke of things they might have had in common with one another in the Living World, though they had never met before.

I let them talk things out. There was no arguing or hostility, so why interrupt them? After all, part of the group sessions was to help the spirits make connections with other souls. However, when their deaths were brought into the conversation, I began paying attention.

"It all happened so fast," one of the ladies said with a sigh. "I woke up in the middle of the street. My body lay on the ground and a crowd gathered around it. This guy was there," she jutted a thumb toward me, "and they were the only one who could see me."

"I'm sorry to hear that," the eldest said, though she had only been in her sixties when she moved on. "For me, I went into surgery and didn't wake up. Well, I did, but with the Grim Reaper."

"Wow," the third soul whistled. "Sounds like you guys had it rough. I kind of knew my time was coming. I got sick a lot, and when I went into the hospital that last time, I had a weird feeling I wouldn't make it out. I did get out, but it was with them." She, too, pointed at me.

They each spoke about me as though I weren't in the room, only casting me quick glances now and then.

"At least you guys saw it coming," one spoke. "I didn't know what happened until I flew through the air from that car."

"I didn't expect to pass away on the operating table," the other replied. "I was nervous about it, but didn't expect it'd happen to me."

"That gut feeling," the third chimed in, agreeing.

The first woman slouched in her seat. "I suspect you guys had friends and family around you. I had strangers who didn't even bother to check for a pulse."

The eldest shook her head. "I died on the operating table. My family was in the waiting room, but we didn't get to say goodbye to each other."

The third woman remained silent. I could tell what she was thinking. She did have her friends around when she moved on. She held her best friend's hand as she exhaled her last breath. She looked at me and muttered, "I guess I did cross the finish line."

"What?" the eldest leaned closer to her.

"I guess I did accomplish what I needed to," she explained. "Even though I don't know what exactly it was." She continued to stare at me, and I nodded reassuringly at her. I didn't know what she accomplished during her time in the Living World. She'd have to think more about it and figure it out herself. She'd get there in time. They all would.

"You were a runner?" the eldest questioned.

She shook her head, chuckling. "No. I don't think I could run if a serial killer chased me."

"Then, what were you talking about?"

"What I spoke about with them during my last session," she explained. "We all walk a different path. We don't know what lies ahead and we don't know how long it'll take us to walk until we actually walk down the road."

"Watch out for the cars ..." the younger woman murmured sarcastically.

"I think, when we die, that means we've crossed the finish line. We won life, so to speak."

"And you're rewarded by getting hit by a car?"

"Well ... I don't know about that one."

The eldest sat taller. "You mean to say that when we accomplish something big in life, something we're meant to do, we die?"

"Yes?" she sounded uncertain.

"Death is the reward?" the third spirit said scornfully. "That's stupid."

The spirit who began the conversation retreated into herself. She looked down at the ground, raising her shoulders into a tight shrug. "Maybe not ... never mind."

The eldest, who sat in between the young women, put one hand on each of the other souls' knees. She looked back and forth between the two with a smile on her face.

"I think it makes sense," she said. "It's part of life. We don't know how much time we have, nor do we know when something will occur for the last time. We live our lives day by day—walking down that path, so to speak—and treat each moment as a learning experience. We take that knowledge with us down the next path, which helps us to keep moving forward."

This pep talk perked up the woman who brought up the conversation. She even made me grin, though I was mostly happy this conversation headed in a positive direction. However, the third woman was unconvinced. She pouted in her seat, not looking at any of us.

"I don't understand why my finish line had to be so early and violent. What did I do to deserve that?"

"No one deserves anything in life," I stated flatly.

All their lives had ended abruptly. Each of them had left behind something important, and none of them had the closure they expected. At least two of these souls were near friends and family at the time of their demise. Having your physical form dropped in the middle of the road with no one around but strangers who didn't know what to do was nerve-wracking. This spirit had every right to be upset about how things ended for her.

"When something negative happens to someone—if they have a stroke of bad luck, for example, they ask themselves, 'What did I do to deserve this?' However, when something positive happens to them, they never question it. Why do you think that is?"

No one answered, yet they all had their undivided attention to me, and I was pleased they were all inclined to listen.

"Everyone has ups and downs in life," I continued. "It may seem like, to you, someone has all the 'luck.' Yet, there are others who can never seem to catch a break. Good and bad happen to everyone—it's a balance. You just don't always notice depending on the situation because you'll see what you want to see."

I looked at the soul to my left. "We talked about that pathway everyone follows. The beginning is similar enough in the sense everyone is born and needs to learn the same skills to grow and keep moving forward. I had mentioned that most people tend to notice when others have crossed their finish line because they're so happy about it. They're proud of themselves. Why do you think you notice when other people find their success and happiness and not yours?"

"Because they're loud about it?" she guessed.

The woman on the right, the one who had been hit by a car, responded. Though she didn't make eye contact with any of us. "Because we're jealous."

I nodded. "It's easiest for us to see what others have rather than see what's right in front of us."

"Why are we like that?" the first soul inquired.

"I think," the eldest replied, holding up a hand and looking at me. I motioned for her to take the floor. "It's because we try to take the easier way. When someone else has what we want, we question how they did it. How did they cross that finish line so fast? How can their story help me with my own? But the reason they crossed their finish line first is because that end was meant for them, not us. We don't see how long it actually took them to get there, we only see the moment it happens and assume the length of time."

"Exactly," I agreed. "You're meant to enjoy your time in the Living World. Have experiences and make memories, but, for some reason, negativity gets mixed in. You'll remember some memories you'd rather forget and forget some memories you'll want to hold close for all eternity."

"Because of the whole balance thing?" the spirit on the left asked.

I nodded.

"You can't have good without the bad, thus positive without negative. Or else the other wouldn't exist." The eldest grinned, catching on. "Otherwise, we wouldn't experience anything."

The Clock glowed orange, as though it were pleased by the conversation. However, I knew the only reason it hadn't ended the session yet was because of the third spirit. She stared absentmindedly out the window, and I frowned. Before I could intervene, the eldest seem to notice how gloomy the other looked, and patted her shoulder comfortingly.

"I don't think the path is always clear," she said. "We don't realize we're walking toward something until we see a glimmer of it. I think that's why, as we grow up, our dreams change. When you're a little girl, you might want to be a ballerina. But, as you get older, you find more things you find interesting. You can still become a ballerina, or you might grow out of that and aim for something else. Whatever that something else is, it'll be better than being a ballerina because it'll be something that's meant for you."

The other soul leaned forward to look around the eldest, facing the other woman. "Where were you going when crossing the street?"

Silence hung in the air for the briefest of moment. The third soul finally turned her head to face all of us, and that's when we all noticed she had been crying.

"I was on my way to quit my job. I had gotten a new one. Something that didn't have to do when my degree. When I told my mother, she thought I was silly. Supportive, yes, but didn't think it was the best move. But it was already done."

"So, you chose the path you wanted over the one you thought you were supposed to do," the eldest recapped encouragingly.

"But I didn't get a chance to walk that new path. I got hit by a car instead," she said somberly.

"What was the job?" I asked, curious.

"I'd train as a curator at an art gallery." She looked right at me, beaming. "I loved painting and always worked on my art during the day. Sometimes late into the night. That's all I wanted to do—create and paint. I had sold a couple of pieces here and there and when the job at the gallery opened up, I ... well, I don't know what came over me. I applied, got an interview, and got an offer. I had no experience, but they were going to take a chance on me, anyway." She sat taller, looking at the rest of the group excitedly. "They even asked to see some of my work so they could display some of it. Isn't that amazing?"

"That is amazing!"

"How wonderful for you!"

"So, you crossed your finish line after all," I said.

She frowned again. "But I didn't get to see the outcome."

"No," I agreed, "but you *know* the outcome. Your finish line was to see if you could make it and ..."

"I did it," she finished my sentence. Her smile came back. "For years, I didn't think I'd be able to make it as an artist, but I could have. I was beginning to, anyway."

"Sometimes the finish line isn't tangible. It's a feeling. All you needed to do was believe in yourself."

GROUP THREE

"Get me out of here."

I stepped back as the newly departed soul charged toward me, avoiding the man. Normally, I didn't get bothered when a soul wanted to leave right away. Yet, when they demanded with such vigor, I couldn't help but be a little stubborn and wonder why.

"What are you waiting for? Stab me! Cut off my head! Do whatever it is you do with that damned weapon!"

My grip tightened on my scythe. "You mean this?"

"That's what I said, isn't it?"

"My scythe isn't a weapon," I corrected him. "Why the rush?"

His shoulders relaxed as he stared at me in confusion. "Are you not the Grim Reaper?"

"I am."

"Then, why linger?"

"Why not?"

He glared at me. I didn't mean to push any buttons, but ... well, here we are.

"I don't want to watch when someone finds me," he said with his voice lowered, as if someone would hear.

I looked down at the body lying on the ground. "What happened?" I asked, even though I already knew. He had tried to hide what he did to make it look like a weird accident. What he probably didn't know was that his family could opt for an autopsy if the cause of death was unknown and sudden. Foul play was indeed involved, but not by the hand of another.

"I ... I don't know. I just did it. Can we get out of here?" the soul asked, desperation hanging on the edge of his tone.

I hesitated. For some reason, I felt like we needed to hang back, even if only for a moment. But I wasn't sure how long it would take for someone to find the body and we couldn't hang around here all day.

Giving in, I held out my hand to bring this spirit to the Afterlife.

"Are you still sleeping, my darling?"

As the door pushed opened to the room, the soul screamed out, and he grabbed my hand before I could take it back.

*

For the longest time, the soul paced the Crossover Room. He didn't sit at the table, didn't touch his beverage, he barely looked at me. I sipped my coffee, sitting back comfortably in my chair. Some sessions were like this. Silence. There wasn't anything I could do or say to get the spirit talking. They always needed to come to me and want to talk.

The fact the spirit had come to the Crossover Room at all was a big step. It meant he had something on his mind, but instantly regretted it the moment he walked in. Unfortunately for him, he didn't realize that once you enter the Crossover Room, you don't leave unless the Clock dismisses you.

And right now, the Clock still shined a bright green.

The soul muttered to himself, still not looking in my direction. He paced, looking down at the ground, twisting his fingers together. Between his confusion, guilt, or regret, and going through the stages of grief, I had a feeling I knew what bothered him so much.

"Would you like to discuss what's on your mind?" I gently asked. Someone had to get the conversation going, but I couldn't force him to talk.

He continued pacing, talking to himself. His voice was low enough that I couldn't make out what he murmured. He paid me no mind, though I didn't know if he didn't hear me or ignored me.

"Whenever you're ready," I said, "I'm here to help. Would you like a drink?" I had made him tea already, but he had refused to come to the table.

Still, no response. It was like I wasn't even in the room.

"Do you wish you could go back?" I asked.

That got his attention. He stopped pacing, stiffened, and stared at me with round, wide eyes. "Back? Where?"

"The Living World," I replied.

"Why would I want to go back there?"

"You seem worried. I didn't know if it was because you missed it."

He sneered at me, turning away and resuming his pacing. "No, no."

"Would you care to elaborate on how you're feeling?" I gently pressed.

"No."

Alright, then. I sighed, sipping my coffee.

"No, no, no ..." he kept muttering.

This session went nowhere fast.

I watched the poor man wander aimlessly around the room, head in his hands, moaning and groaning. He was clearly in agony, and I didn't know how to help. Not without him talking to me. Whatever his reasoning was for wanting to leave the Living World so soon was beyond my comprehension. His internal clock had reached zero, yes, though he didn't know that.

I didn't know anything about the souls I brought to the Afterlife. All I knew was how they died and what happened to them a few minutes before they exited their physical form. I often knew more about how they moved on without some of the spirits knowing themselves. Even in death, the mind had a funny way of playing tricks. If the death was too traumatic, the soul would believe anything else other than the truth.

In this case, I had a feeling he remembered what happened. He knew what he did. Now whether he regretted it, I wasn't sure. Did he think it was all a dream, and he'd wake up back in the Living World? Did he think his plan didn't work? Now he was here and couldn't go back. Did he feel stuck?

Stuck like he did in the Living World, no doubt.

But now he was here in the Afterlife, here to stay until his next life. Was there no escape for him?

"No, no, no ..." he moaned, wiping away tears, rubbing his face with his hands. The turmoil on his face was almost unbearable to witness. If he weren't already dead, I would have thought he'd give himself a heart attack from stress.

Unfortunately, he wasn't the first soul to arrive here by their own hand. Sometimes, the spirit was relieved. Sometimes, they mourned their previous life and their loved ones. Others regretted their actions upon arriving here.

"Why do I still feel like this?" he demanded, his voice slicing through the air.

"Feel like what?" I asked.

Sure, it was a dumb question. He clearly was distraught, hurt, regretful, confused, angry ... there were too many emotions weighing heavily on his mind. But which emotion was I meant to tackle first?

"I thought I'd feel better!" he shouted. "Why do I still feel lousy? I hurt, but I don't know why."

"Where does it hurt?" I asked calmly. Spirits couldn't feel physical pain, but I needed him to keep talking to me, hoping he'd eventually admit his feelings.

"Everywhere!" he screeched, wildly throwing his arms about, pointing all over his body.

I remained steady. "Why do you suppose you hurt everywhere?"

"I don't know!" he screamed again. Quieter, he added, "I thought if I left, I'd feel better ... if I let everything go ... things might be better ... without me."

I stood as he dropped to his knees.

"But I'm still stressed. I'm still sad. I'm still ..."

"Please," I calmly interrupted, "join me at the table. I want to help you."

"Everything hurts," he said, looking up at me. He pressed his palms against his chest. "My insides feel tight. My body's heavy. I'm suffocating."

He didn't have insides anymore. All he had were his memories of his previous life. The only way he'd feel better was if he found his peace, but that wouldn't happen if he regretted his time in the Living World. But how do I explain this delicately?

I walked around to the other side of the table, standing above him. Before I could speak, he folded his hands together, begging.

"Please, end it."

"End what?"

"Me. I thought I died, but I'm still here."

"You're in the Afterlife. Whatever you did, you succeeded."

"Then, why do I still feel this way?"

I frowned, wishing I could make his pain go away. Much like in the Living World, that's not how things worked in the Afterlife. I couldn't wave a magic wand and make his problems disappear. I was a guide, nothing more.

"Come," I said, pointing to the table. "Let's sit together."

I was surprised when he stood, though it was slow. First one leg, then the other, and he pushed his legs to straighten as they shook in a standing position, as though he carried a boulder on his shoulders.

I turned to walk back to the table, looking over my shoulder to ensure he followed. He didn't. Instead, his eyes glazed over to the ground.

"Did it help anyone?" he murmured, his tone faraway in a trance.

I paused, turning to face him. "Who?"

"Everyone."

I shook my head. "I'm not sure I can answer that for you. If you have any loved ones you'd like to check in on, you can—"

"No."

I closed my mouth as he balled his hands into fists.

"All I did was cause issues." His voice shook. "I was a burden. I couldn't help myself. I couldn't help them. That's why I ... it's why I had to ... because if I didn't ..." his body collapsed onto the ground again.

I picked up his tea and brought it over to him. "Let's take a moment."

He ignored me and the tea, putting his head in his hands. "What was my life? I didn't amount to anything. I didn't help anyone. I didn't do anything meaningful. Trouble. That's all I did. Cause trouble. Brought on pain. I wasn't any good."

I absorbed his frantic words, unsure of what trials and tribulations this man had faced in the Living World. He truly was a tortured soul. The worst I'd seen in a while.

"That's why I had to leave. I had to go. If I didn't, then ..."

I sat down on the floor beside him, resting his teacup on my knee. "What would have happened if you stayed?" I was sure he wasn't as alone as he thought he was, positive he was loved more than he knew.

He looked at me, panic-stricken. "If I stayed, then ... nothing would have changed. I still would have caused trouble and everyone ... they would have ..."

"Who would have been there for you?" I pressed, attempting to change this conversation's direction.

"I don't—"

"You know who," I didn't let him finish. "You know why, too."

He sniffled, shoulders shaking as he began crying. I noticed he eyed the tea but didn't reach for it.

"Whatever you thought before was a lie. You had people who cared about you, who loved you. They wanted to see you succeed," I said in a delicate tone, but firm enough to get my message across. "Your life was important. You mattered."

He looked at me through wet, bloodshot eyes. "I didn't want to see her find me ... I didn't want to see everyone's reactions when they heard the news. I loved them all."

"And they loved you in return," I replied reassuringly.

"Is that why I don't feel any better?"

I hesitated. "Maybe."

No matter how it ended, his time was up. His internal clock reached zero, so whether he did it himself or something else happened, we'd be sitting here together in the Afterlife, regardless. Why it needed to be this way, I wasn't sure. I didn't know anything about this man, but I knew enough to know that he didn't deserve these harsh feelings.

It was never an easy conversation to have. Every spirit was different, no matter how similar their tales may be. Even if their deaths were caused by the same thing, or they arrived at the Afterlife at the same age, their time in the Living World was vastly different from one another.

Some I could talk off a ledge, others figured it out for themselves. Some didn't need a talking to at all, and others were relieved to be in the Spirit World. They were the ones satisfied with the memories they carried. There would always be the occasional soul who hurt so bad, I knew they'd be in the Afterlife for a while before moving on.

Much like the amount of time souls had in the Living World, it was unclear why some lingered longer than others in between lives.

The spirit abruptly stood up, turning his back to me.

I hurt alongside him. I felt helpless. I was the Grim Reaper, supposed to help.

He walked over to the window, leaned over it, and stuck his head into the void.

So, why were there times when I had no idea what to do or say?

He screamed. His scream pierced the room, growing louder. It was deafening, overpowering the darkness that surrounded us. The abyss didn't echo back.

I stood, teacup in hand, and watched him. Listened.

He screamed until he couldn't any longer.

For the first time, I had no words of comfort.

When he looked like he was about to collapse from exhaustion, the Clock turned red.

I had met souls all over. It could have been their home, a friend's house, a medical center, a birthday party ... the stories I could recount are endless. A spirit may return to the Afterlife at any time, no matter what their physical form is doing or where they are.

Depending on the place, the soul was almost always aware they were dead. They'd be in denial most of the time, but even they couldn't ignore the out-of-body experience.

For this spirit, I was brought to a beautiful backyard. Rows of flowers lined the perimeter of the yard, and in the middle was a lush vegetable garden. The Spirit World doesn't follow a calendar or have seasons like the Living World does, but I could guess this area was experiencing late spring or early summer. I blinked up at the shining sun, knowing how I should feel right now, but I couldn't remember what the sun's rays felt like.

It took me longer than I care to admit to find the spirit. They were deep in their garden, kneeling beside a flower bed. Their back was to me, so I didn't think they knew I had arrived.

"I don't understand," I heard them mutter.

I stepped closer, looking over their shoulder. A small gardening shovel lay on the ground. They tried picking it up, but to no avail. I looked around the yard, wondering where their physical form lay. Clearly, they hadn't realized they were dead.

"Why won't my hands work?" they kept muttering to themselves, still unaware of my presence.

"Excuse me?" I piped up.

They looked up, tilting their head backward to stare at me upside down. "Oh, hello."

"Hello," I said. "What are you doing there?"

"Gardening." The response was blunt as they turned their attention back to the shovel. "My hands won't work." They tried to pick the shovel up again, but their transparent fingers went right through the tool and into the ground. "See?" They looked at me again as though I could fix it.

"I'm sorry you're struggling. Why don't we—"

"Can you fix it?"

"Fix it?"

"You're the Grim Reaper?"

"Well, yeah, but—"

"Then can you help me plant these seeds before we go?"

So, they knew they were dead. When I didn't answer right away, they continued.

"I bought these seeds the other day and I don't want them to go to waste. It'd be a shame for these flowers not to have the chance to live."

I frowned. I could pull some strings in the Afterlife, but the Living World? Not so much. "I'm sorry," I said. "Unfortunately, I don't have the authority to do that here."

"Who does?" they asked.

"I mean, I don't have the power to garden here."

"Why not?"

"I'm not a physical being."

They cocked their head to the side. "But you're holding your scythe."

I glanced at my scythe as though it had tattled on me. "That's different."

"How?"

I didn't have an answer for that.

They sighed, standing to their feet. "Alright, if there's nothing I can do, then let's go."

I nodded. "So, you know you've moved on?"

"Yes. Two days ago now."

I inaudibly gasped. Rarely was I late to pick up a soul, and even I couldn't explain why. Maybe it was a backlog of souls moving on at once, or maybe some of those spirits were stronger than I realized.

"Have you been trying to plant those seeds all this time?"

They nodded.

"What about your physical form?" I imagined their family and friends already called the authorities to take it away. They had to have died at home or else they wouldn't be in this spot.

"It's in my bed," they said, pointing to their house.

My jaw dropped. "Still?"

"No one's come by to say hello," they shrugged. They started walking away, looking all around with their hands on their hips. "Which way do we go?"

I sighed, hoping to see this soul in the Crossover Room soon. "Take my hand," I said, stretching out my arm.

They looked over their shoulder. "But my hands don't work."

"They will for this."

*

A blue rose in a tall skinny vase sat in the center of the table. It never needed watering, never wilted. It didn't have a scent. When another soul complained about the dreariness of the Crossover Room, I created the blue flower. It was the first thing that came to mind. Simple, but I liked it.

Why shouldn't the room have a homier ambiance? Why shouldn't it be more comforting? For me and for the spirits that come here.

Yet, the blue flower was an odd reminder that I was always here. Spirits come and go, but I'll always be here.

Anyway, this isn't about me. The soul sitting across the table glared at the blue flower, and I'll admit, it rubbed me the wrong way. I created it and this spirit loved gardening, so I couldn't understand why they would dislike my rose.

They had refused a beverage—even hot chocolate. I didn't give myself a drink, so I didn't seem rude, but now I didn't know what to do with myself. We sat in silence for a long time, with them glaring harshly at my flower, unblinking.

"Do you like it?" I asked.

No response. Not even a flinch.

The Clock on the wall was still green. I leaned back in my chair, trying not to seem impatient.

After another moment, they leaned forward, resting their chin on the surface of the table. Their eyes locked with the vase, brows furrowed. Why were they thinking? They no longer looked angry, but highly interested in it. If I had known a flower would have made such an impact, I might not have had it at all. Unless it was a positive impact.

Even though they looked upset by it before, now they rested their chin in the crook of their elbows, resting their head like a child by a window, waiting to catch a glimpse of Santa Claus.

That thought made me wonder. I changed the color of the flower to pink.

The spirit's eyes widened, impressed. Dare I say I detected a slight smile on their face?

I changed the color to yellow. Yes, there was a grin on their face.

Green, red, orange, and then, finally, rainbow. Every petal a different, bright color.

The spirit sat tall, giggling.

"Do you like it?" I asked again.

They nodded. "I've never seen anything like it. What flower shop did you get it from?"

I shook my head. "No flower shop here. I made it myself."

"You grew it in your garden?"

"Sure."

"You've got one hell of a green thumb." They rested their chin on the table again, starting at the colorful petals.

"Did you like flowers in the Living World?" I questioned, already knowing the answer.

"I had a garden in my backyard," they answered. "Had a greenhouse and everything. I grew lots of things. Vegetables, fruits, flowers. If you can stick it in the ground and grow something new, you bet that's what I did. Bringing something to life is an amazing feeling."

"I bet it is."

"Well, you should know." They lifted their head, finally looked at me. "You grew this."

"I did." I didn't. Not technically, anyway. But I'd let them think that for the sake of the conversation.

"Gardening made me so happy," they continued without prompting. "Plants are living creatures, you know."

"They are," I agreed.

"They breathe like we do. Drink water and soak up vitamin D whenever they can. Most plants are smart enough to grow toward the sun. Did you know that?"

I did, but pretended not to. "That's amazing."

"They don't have the same worries and stresses as humans."

Unless they had a human who forgot to water them, but I nodded along.

"They're only focus is to grow. Better themselves."

I smirked, liking where this conversation headed.

"I think all humans can learn from plants. Some are prickly, some aren't. Others have beautiful colors and some are quite dull. But they all have personality and keep growing. It's so cool!"

"It absolutely is. I've never thought about plants like that before."

"Some smell great and others don't. You can eat some of them, too, but I don't think they'd appreciate that much."

A chuckle escaped my lips. "I wouldn't imagine so, no."

"I wanted to keep growing. Just like the plants in my garden." Their tone changed, so mine did, too.

"Did you?"

They frowned. "I don't know. If you asked my friends or family, they'd probably tell you no. I think I did, but it was hard for me to go out of my comfort zone. Did you know plants grow best when in their particular zone? It's called a hardiness zone. It tracks the areas for weather conditions, temperature, soil, and things like that so you know which parts of the world would be best to grow a certain plant. Well, my hardiness zone was my house. My backyard."

I pressed my lips into a smile. The way they spoke and compared everything to plants was sweet. Yet, there was rejection in their tone, as if this conversation was difficult for them to admit.

"I tried. Really, I did," they said. "I kept myself fed and watered. I had good hygiene. I spent a lot of time in the sun—tending to my garden, of course. But some people didn't think that was right for me. They wanted me to go out and meet new people. But then they'd complain when I'd meet new people and talk about my garden."

"Would you change anything about your life?" I questioned.

"No."

"You were happy?"

"Of course. That's why I don't know why they cared so much. I did what I liked. What's wrong with that?"

"Absolutely nothing," I said reassuringly. "I wouldn't worry too much about what others think."

They cracked a smile. "Oh, I don't worry about that. Plants have no worries, so why should I? It's the only way to live life well. Take things day by day. Be kind to your neighbors. Companion planting is important."

No matter what was on this spirit's mind, plants always found a way to sneak into the conversation. Even I hadn't realized how much plants could teach us about living.

"I'm glad to see you have flowers here. No offense, but it's kind of dreary," they said. Casting me a shy grin. "Having flowers out and about might help some of the souls here feel better. More comfortable."

"That's what I was going for," I agreed.

The Clock turned red, and I realized I didn't notice the sessions neared its end. I didn't know why this soul had come to me because it seemed they were completely fine with their situation. It's didn't bother me, though. I was happy to have a positive conversation with them, not having to fix any problems and explain too deeply about life and death.

As I watched them leave the room, I couldn't help but wonder—and hope—that someone in the Living World continued to care for their garden.

The house was a mess, its floor covered with trash and dirty clothes, and the couch was visibly filthy. I didn't want to think about what caused those stains. Normally, I appeared to where the body lay. However, I wasn't able to tell where anything was in this person's living room. I hoped it wasn't buried underneath the trash.

"Who are you?"

I looked up from the floor, the voice breaking me from my judgmental thoughts. Embarrassed at my thinking, even though they couldn't read my mind, I cleared my throat before answering.

"I'm the Grim Reaper."

"Why are you here?" the spirit questioned from the doorway to another room.

"I'm here to bring you home."

"This is my home."

"Your new home," I amended. Maybe he didn't realize he was dead.

He looked around the room, casting his gaze up at the ceiling, then down to the floor. He looked over his shoulder before staring at me quizzically again. Then he shrugged his shoulders as though he answered me, but I didn't say anything.

I stepped forward, but he stepped back, as though he were my mirror. So, I stopped, and he stopped, too, still an equal distance away from one another.

"Are you the only one who came?" he asked.

I nodded, and he frowned.

"Were you expecting company?" I took this as an opportunity to step closer again. He didn't seem to notice, so I kept stepping forward until he looked up at me again.

"No, I wasn't," he drawled. He bowed his head once more, so I took another step.

"Is there something I can help with?" Another step.

The spirit looked up, shocked to see how much closer I was to him. He didn't recoil away, but stared with wide eyes. "I ... I don't think so," he said, quietly.

I reached out a hand. "Then, why don't we head home?"

He looked around the area, confused. "But I already told you. This is my home."

"It was," I corrected.

"What happened to me?"

"You died."

"When?"

"Not long ago."

"Here?"

"Yes."

After a moment of letting my words sink in, he stretched his hand out, hovering his palm over mine. I remained still, allowing him to be the one to transport us to the Afterlife once he was ready.

Looking me in the eye, he asked, "Where's home?"

"The Afterlife," I answered as he gently pressed his palm to mine.

*

"Coffee? Tea?" I asked.

The spirit sat at the table, slouched down with his shoulders hunched over and his arms crossed. He sat rigid, not looking at me. "You can get that here?" he murmured.

"I can make it happen."

"Coffee."

I made two mugs appear on the table—coffee for him, and coffee for me. Picking up my mug, I took a sip, letting the hot liquid scorch my tongue. It was the only time I could feel something in the Spirit World.

Over the rim of my cup, I watched carefully as the spirit sat taller in his chair. He reached out for his cup, cautiously picking it up. He inspected it, bringing it close to his face. It was like he wondered whether it was real. Or maybe he thought it was poison. I continued to drink mine, not wanting to interrupt his thoughts. When he brought the cup to his lips and took a sip, I grinned as his eyes sparkled at the taste.

"Good?" I asked.

He nodded, still gulping down the beverage.

After giving him another minute, I put my cup on the table, leaning forward a tad. "Did you want to talk about anything?"

He swallowed, lowering his mug, but still holding it tight with both hands. "Why is this so good?"

I smiled. "I guess I just make it well, not to toot my own horn."

What the souls didn't know was that the beverages tasted different to everyone. Each time a soul had asked for coffee, tea, or hot chocolate, it tasted like their favorite cup—however they liked to enjoy it in the Living World. Essentially, it was a memory.

"Well, you do a fabulous job, whatever it is," he chuckled. "I don't know how you did it, but it's tastes like …" he paused.

After a moment of silence, I pressed him further. "Tastes like that?"

He lifted his chin, deep in thought. "It tastes like home."

"I assume that's a good thing?"

"It's excellent."

"Good."

"But …" he sighed, putting the mug down. That's when I noticed he drank it all.

When he didn't complete his thought, I pointed to his drink. "Refill?"

He pushed it closer to me and I added more. Without hesitation, he grabbed it with both hands again, sipping more. He retreated further into his chair, sighing contentedly.

"I'm glad you enjoy it so much," I said, "but was there something you wanted to say?"

The spirit opened his eyes more, almost as if he forgot the conversation was about to start. He sat up again, looking out into the void through the window. "Well, I was going to say that this reminding me of home is bittersweet."

I nodded, silently hoping he'd continued. Thankfully, he did.

"Not because I can't be there anymore," he clarified, "but because I was alone."

"You lived alone, you mean?" I questioned.

He nodded. "But it's not just that. I didn't have anyone. No one came to check on me at all. That's why, when I saw you, I was confused. Who would come to visit me?"

I frowned, keeping quiet.

"It sounds weird, but I was a little excited to see that someone had visited me. I got happy to see you, even though you were only there because I died. Is that weird of me?"

"I don't think so," I said, shaking my head. "All of us want to have company once in a while. We all get lonely. Sometimes the company of a stranger is exactly what we need."

The soul let out a light chuckle while shaking his head. "I was a bit of a loner. I wanted the company, yeah, but whenever I had the opportunity to be around others, I suddenly didn't want anything to do with them anymore. It made me nervous. I didn't know how to interact with people. Not since I had lost my best friend."

"Everyone reacts to change differently, and we all grieve in our own ways, too," I remarked.

"My friend was the social one," he continued. "He made friends easily, and I tagged along. He never seemed to mind. And then ... when they died, I was alone. I fell out of touch with all the people I had connected to through my friend. I wanted to reach out to those people, but I couldn't bring myself to do it. I don't know if it was grief or nerves or something else."

"Did anyone reach out to you?"

"There was one. They reached out a couple of times, but I could never bring myself to answer the phone. Eventually, they stopped. They must have thought I hated them. Or maybe they thought I only hung out with them because of our mutual friend."

"I'm sure they didn't think that," I countered. "I imagine they understood you weren't ready to reach out yet. They probably thought you'd reach out when you were ready."

"But I was never ready."

"No, but I don't think they'd hold that against you."

He opened his mouth but promptly closed it again. Confused, I glanced at the Clock—which was still green—before turning my attention back to the soul.

"What's that?" he asked, pointing to the Clock.

"It keeps track of our session time," I stated.

"It doesn't have a face, though."

"No, it doesn't."

"How much time do we have left?"

"I don't know."

"You can't read it?"

"No one can."

"Then how ...?"

"Tell me about this friend of yours," I said, changing the subject. "The one who moved on."

He sighed, resting his back against his chair. He didn't seem to mind the topic change, nor did he seem to mind being asked about his departed friend. "I don't know what to say. He was a great guy, helping me with so much. I wasn't a great human being, you know."

"No?" I prompted for more information.

"I don't mean bad or anything like that," he explained. "I just mean I wasn't great at taking care of myself. I struggled a lot, mentally and physically. I kept to myself, but couldn't find the motivation to care for myself, to care for my living space."

I nodded along, listening intently.

"My friend hired a cleaning service for me. I felt so guilty letting people see that part of me. It was weird not being able to do it myself. But my friend didn't seem to mind at all and neither did the cleaning service. Although, they probably loved the business. But it was odd having a friend pay for something like that. I offered to pay him back many times, but he always refused. He knew I struggled to go to work most days, so he told me to save my paychecks for bills and groceries."

I grinned. "It sounds like he cared a lot about you."

"He did, and I didn't give him anything in return."

"I'm sure that's not true."

"It is."

"What about your friendship?"

"I couldn't pay for things like he did for me. Whenever we went out, he'd always pay for me."

"He wouldn't have done that if he didn't want to," I stated. "I don't think he would have kept hanging out with you if he thought you were such a burden."

For some reason, that statement got him to laugh. "I guess not, but I still would have liked to do something for him. At the very least, I could have kept my place clean after he passed away. I couldn't keep the cleaning service because I couldn't afford it. They offered to do it for a discount, but I declined. The offer was nice of them, but they worked too hard for me not to pay full price."

"It sounds like they cared about you, too," I added. "It's rare a business would go above and beyond for one of their customers. They knew you were in a tight spot, and I'm sure once they noticed you grieving, that was their way of helping."

The spirit grunted, slinking his chair. "Oh great, now it looks like I can't even be grateful for help."

I laughed, which caused him to retreat further into his chair, embarrassed. "That's not what I meant. I'm merely pointing out to you that there were people around you that cared about your wellbeing. You weren't as alone as you think."

He stared at me with wide eyes, sitting taller again. He peered out the window and then back at me. "You really think so?"

"I know so."

The Clock turned orange. I didn't know if what I said changed his perspective, or if he had just needed a little reassurance.

Glancing at the Clock, I noticed he saw it change, catching on to how it worked. He stood, ready to dismiss himself.

"I was excited when you arrived because I thought someone visited me," he repeated. "I don't know who is going to find my body in my house. I never got visitors. My corpse might be laying in my house for weeks before anyone notices I'm gone." He began walking out of the Crossover Room, and as he got closer to the door, the Clock turned red.

I frowned, not having a response for him. Unfortunately, that happened more often than one would think. It's important to reach out to those you care about today rather than waiting for tomorrow. You never know what tomorrow will bring for you, or for them. But this wasn't the right time for me to say that to him now.

The three souls inhabiting the Crossover Room with me stood far apart from one another, almost if it they all believe the others were contagious. The first soul walked to the other side of the room, bypassing the table where I sat. He stood by the window, watching the emptiness. After him, the second soul entered the room cautiously. However, when they noticed the rainbow rose still in the center of the table, they skipped over to the table, smiling at the flower as they had before. Finally, the third spirit appeared. He looked around warily, not paying anyone any attention. He came over to the table, but when he noticed the middle seat was taken and his only option was to sit beside someone else, he stood away from the table instead.

I waved a friendly hand. "Won't you join us?"

His hesitation lasted so long, I thought he'd refuse. Instead, he stiffly put one foot in front of the other and made his way over to the table. He sat down in the chair to my left, closest to the door. I assumed he'd want a quick getaway, even though he wouldn't be able to leave without the Clock dismissing him. The Clock had already turned green, which meant the session had begun. Although, not everyone was seated at the table.

Casting a glance at the third soul, I noticed he was silently crying by the window. I frowned, wondering if it was too soon to invite him to a group session. I decided not to coax him over to the table just yet.

"Would anyone like a drink?" I asked the other two, but neither answered. "Is there anything anyone would like to share?" I questioned encouragingly.

Still no answer.

I leaned forward on the table, staring at the soul who watched the rose gracefully. They would help get the session going, I was sure of it.

"Do you still like it?" I asked.

They nodded, their eyes finally looking past the flower and at me instead.

"Did you want to talk about the flower?" I pressed.

They sat up, curious. "Did you grow more?"

"No, this is it."

"Why didn't you grow more?"

I shrugged. "This was all I could come up with." I was sure I could create a bouquet, but the one rose seemed to be enough for now.

The spirit frowned. "Oh, I see. Sometimes it's hard to get flowers to grow."

"Oh, really?" I asked, intrigued.

They nodded. "All plants have the same needs—water, sun, good companions ... but they need varying levels of those needs. Some plants need to be watered once a week while others urge for a sip every day. Then you have plants that need sunlight all day and others only want a little before cooling off in the shade for the rest of the day. Then you have some plants that fight."

"Fight?" I echoed. This conversation took a turn.

"Uh-huh," they said in a serious tone. "If you don't plant the right companions near them, it can stunt their growth. There are some plants, like mint, that will take over the entire garden!" They threw their arms up briefly to gesture just how much mint can take over. They put their arms back down gently. "That's why you need to surround yourself with others who care about your growth just as much as their own. Some people are like mint and will try to push you away so they can have all the legroom and sun."

The spirit sitting beside them ducked when their arms flailed about. He straightened himself out in his seat once he was no longer in the hazard zone. "What did you just say?"

"Mint can be mean," they replied nonchalantly.

"No," he groaned, "the other thing. About the right companions?"

"About how some plants grow better around other certain plants?"

"Yes. You said if you place two incompatible plants together, they could stunt each other's growth?"

"Yep."

"Interesting." He looked away.

I remained quiet through the interaction, silently begging for them to continue. When the conversation abruptly ended, I spoke up. "Did you want to add anything?"

The soul shook his head, but the gardener leaned closer to him, grinning.

"Did you like gardening, too?" they asked.

"Not really," he replied curtly.

"Oh."

Seeing the dejected expression on their face, he amended his statement. "I mean, I never tried it before."

The spirit beside him perked up once more. "Oh, it's wonderful! I could teach you if you want."

"There are gardens here?" he looked away from them and turned to me instead.

I shook my head.

"We can talk about it!" the gardener exclaimed.

The other spirit looked overwhelmed, but they didn't recoil away. "You'd want to talk about it? With me?"

"Why not?"

He couldn't answer that. Instead, he sheepishly turned his gaze back to the ground. Not understanding his body language, the other soul continued speaking about plants, further explaining companion planting. To my relief, the soul beside him listened.

I took this as an opportunity to stand, and walked over to the third spirit still by the window. Not once had he looked over his shoulder to face the group, but he must have heard us.

He didn't seem to notice me standing beside him. I followed his distant gaze out the window, not seeing anything. I often wondered what souls saw out the window. To me, it was an abyss. To them, it might have been something more. Maybe it was just a quiet place for them to get lost in their thoughts.

If that were the case, I didn't want to interrupt. This spirit had been so tortured by his time in the Living World—or by himself, I wasn't sure which—I was afraid he'd shut down completely if I spoke. It wasn't often I was speechless when helping souls move forward, but there were times when I was at a complete loss for how to help.

Before I could muster the courage to say anything to him, the gardener emerged from the other side of him, frightening him.

"Hey!" they exclaimed. "Did you want to talk about plants? We're talking about companion planting."

Unsure, he looked over his shoulder at the other soul, who remained at the table. He shrugged and I couldn't help but smirk at how these two connected, because one of them had a fixation on plants.

But then the spirit looked at me, as though seeking guidance. I finally saw it. I saw the deep sadness in his eyes, dark and hollow. Just like the window.

"Go ahead," I managed to say, the words coming out as a rasp. I nodded my head to the table, silently encouraging him to sit.

Before he could react, the gardener grabbed him by the hand, excited that their hands worked here. The other spirit flinched, but didn't fight back. Instead, he allowed himself to be lured to the table. The gardener sat in the middle seat, and the other soul sat beside him in the remaining chair. The table was finally filled. Well, except for me. But I stayed by the window, afraid that if I moved, I'd ruin the moment.

"This is so exciting! In the Living World, I had trouble making friends, but today is so easy," they exclaimed.

I grinned, watching how happy they were. Even the other two souls cracked smiles, though neither of them spoke.

The gardener kept filling the silence. "I always wanted to talk about my plants and it annoyed people so much that they didn't want to talk to me anymore." They turned their head left and right to ensure they spoke to both spirits sitting on either side of them. "But you guys don't seem to mind at all! You even asked me to explain more. No one has ever asked me about my plants before."

The spirit sitting to their right, who was shy until now, slightly raised his hand to speak. "I didn't know what companion planting was, and I'm still not sure I get it. But something you said resonated with me. I always had trouble making friends, too. I had one who was so kind to me. They took care of me and were always so patient whenever I felt stuck."

"Gardening takes a lot of patience," they replied. "You can't rush growth. I think that friends of yours was a good companion for you."

"But I don't think I was a good companion for them," he countered.

"Of course you were."

"How do you know?"

"Companion plants grow well *together*. Helping you was a way that helped them grow, thus you grew. Plants are smart. They grow toward what helps them. What makes them feel good."

He sat back in his chair, relieved. "I never thought about it that way before. So, even though I didn't give anything in return, you really think I helped him grow?"

"You gave him your friendship. Not many people know how to ask for help and you accepted it from him. You must have really trusted him, and he must have really loved you." The gardener explained it so simply.

That made the other spirit smile. He sat taller, patting the soul beside him on the shoulder as a brief thanks, but too choked up to speak the words out loud.

"Wait," the third spirit spoke up. I froze, eager to hear what he had to say. "What about me?"

"What about you?" the gardener responded so bluntly, I winced. Thankfully, the other spirit didn't seem to mind.

"Did I ... you know, have companion plants around me?"

"I don't know, did you?"

Silence filled the room as I bit my tongue. These spirits didn't know one another when they were in the Living World. They barely knew each other now. The gardener had explained it so eloquently to the other soul without knowing anything about the third. I hoped they'd share the same words of wisdom with this poor soul. He needed a pep talk, and so far, I haven't been able to get through to him.

But then I noticed how deep in thought he was. For once, he wasn't blanketed in grief and regret. Not only did the gardener manage to bring him to the table, but they encouraged him to join the conversation.

He finally stammered out a response. "I ... I think so."

"Of course you did!" the gardener beamed. "How else would you have made it so far?"

They rendered the rest of us speechless. When none of us answered, they spoke again.

"We don't get far in life without the companion of others. I loved my plants, but I know I wouldn't have been able to get where I was in life if it wasn't for the humans who loved me."

One soul smiled at them. "You're right. Those who love you help you love yourself. You can help them do the same. We probably all did that without realizing it."

The other spirit shook his head. "I didn't. I always caused trouble for everyone."

The gardener, still holding the hands of the others, turned their body to face him. "Did you know that when roots get blocked by rocks or something underground, they'll move around it?"

"Uh ... cool," he replied, confusion edging his tone.

"Even plants get stuck sometimes. We all do. We get blocked, but then can think our way around the problem to move forward."

"Are we still talking about plants?" the other soul questioned.

The gardener looked over their shoulder. "We're always talking about plants." They turned their attention back to the other spirit in front of them. "The roots grow deep so the rest of themselves—the stem, petals—can grow tall and bloom. It takes a lot of work from the inside to grow, and not everyone will see. You might not even see it yourself, but there are people around you that notice the hard work you put in. They see you growing and they're cheering you on. That's why they chose to grow alongside you. That's why you're their companion plant."

The other two spirits exchanged glances, tears forming on both their faces. The gardener frowned, looking back and forth between the two before settling a confused expression on me.

"Did I say something wrong?" they asked.

I smiled at them. They were so ignorant of their wisdom. "No," I said, shaking my head. "I think your words were just right."

The spirit who arrived in the Afterlife by his own hand burst into tears. He grabbed the gardener, wrapping him in a tight hug.

Shock flashed in the gardener's eyes, but only for a moment. He smiled warmly and hugged back, with his eyes closed. The third spirit wiped away his own tears before standing to face me.

"I need to find my friend. He died a few years ago, will he be here?"

"Of course. You won't have to look hard. I'm sure he's looking for you, too," I answered.

The Clock turned red, and the spirit said his thanks to the gardener before leaving.

Standing, the other spirit rushed over to me. "I need to go back. I need to apologize to them. I didn't see it before, I didn't ..."

I put a hand on their shoulder. "It's okay," I whispered. "They know. I can't bring you back to life, but you can head to the Living World whenever you want to check on them."

"But I need to tell them."

"You'll find a way."

For the first time, he smiled. He ran out of the Crossover Room, eager to find his loved ones.

Finally, I turned to the gardener, pleased at how this session went and I only had them to thank for it. Before I could say anything, though, they stared at me with the goofiest grin you ever did see.

They stuck out their hand toward me, their tone warm. "Thank you for finding me some friends."

I shook their hand, my tone heartfelt. "Thank you for helping them grow."

The Beginning of the End

Rarely did I have a moment to myself in the Crossover Room, for I had little downtime in between spirits. If no one needed a session, then I'd be in the Living World bringing more souls over to the Afterlife.

So, you can imagine my confusion when nothing happened.

The Clock glowed yellow throughout the room, which typically meant a soul waited for a session. Yet, no one entered the room when I let them in, nor was I summoned to the Living World.

Was it odd? Absolutely. Unsettling? A little. However, I'd be lying if I said I didn't enjoy relishing in the warm glow of the Clock. The Afterlife was so dark all the time. I was used to it, of course, and I didn't mind the dark. Yet, the glow was nice.

I didn't know why the Clock changed only to certain colors. I also didn't know why it changed in the first place during these sessions. After all the time I've spent in the Spirit World, one would think I'd understand how the Afterlife works. Unfortunately, I was in the dark just as much as the spirits I brought here.

A soul had once asked if the Afterlife was a safe space. I answered immediately, saying that it was. At least, I never had trouble here, and as far as I was concerned, none of the other souls who inhabited the Spirit World had any trouble. We helped each other, took care of one another in ways they never did in the Living World.

The Afterlife felt eerie at times, but it was oddly comforting. The yellow light illuminating from the Clock was no sunrise, but it was the closest I'd ever get to it. It never emitted warmth, but I could close my eyes and imagine it.

The problem was, I couldn't tell if what I imagined was real. I couldn't remember what it felt like to be warm. I've been in the Afterlife for … well, how long has it been? Time didn't exist here. Not in the way it did in the Living World.

How did I get here? A spirit had asked me that once. Another spirit had asked how I got this "job." Was it a job? I didn't get paid, but currency didn't exist in the Spirit World. The question didn't bother me so much, but my lack of an answer did.

So, how did I become the Grim Reaper? Was I always like this? Did I ever get a turn experiencing the Living World? Was I ever alive?

Why am I questioning my existence?

I looked at the Clock once more, tuning into the yellow haze that covered the room. I knew how the Afterlife worked, for the most part. I didn't have all the answers, but I knew enough. But I couldn't understand why the Clock was stuck on yellow. Was it broken?

Standing from my chair, I walked over to the doorway, but it was still empty. Not a soul to be found. I craned my neck upward to look at the Clock directly above the archway. The yellow seemed harsher from this spot.

I cast a calm gaze over my shoulder at the table. My scythe leaned against the chair I normally sat in. It didn't radiate at all, so I knew no souls were waiting for me in the Living World. It was odd, since multiple souls moved on every second.

It wasn't like me to fret, but now I worried something was truly wrong. No spirits waited outside the Crossover Room and no souls waited in the Living World. Yet the Clock knew someone was waiting. Where were they?

I thought of two explanations. One, the Clock had malfunctioned, and I had no idea how to fix it. That was one of the hardest things about being the Grim Reaper. It was just me. I didn't have any co-workers or a boss to help me out around here. I was alone and needed to rely on myself to understand everything.

Two, the Clock was completely fine, and I was losing my touch.

I stiffened at the thought. No, that couldn't be it. Who was the Grim Reaper if they couldn't help spirits in need? What would I be if I weren't the Grim Reaper?

I staggered back to the small, round table. I stared at the rainbow rose sitting pretty as a centerpiece. I hadn't noticed it before, but its petals faced the chair where the souls normally sat. I remember seeing it facing me last time.

Maybe I really was losing my touch.

I was about to sit back down when something in my gut, despite not having one, told me not to sit there. I couldn't put my finger on it. I had never had this feeling before. What did it mean? What was I supposed to do about it?

My head turned, looking at the seat opposite where I usually sat. It was the chair souls used when they needed to get something off their chest. When they needed help with understanding. Guidance.

What would happen if I sat in that seat? I've never done it before. I didn't need guidance, but it was just a chair, so what did it matter if I sat on the left instead of the right?

I side-stepped twice to my left, staring down at the chair. It was already pulled out from the table, as though it was inviting me to sit. Slowly, I bent my knees.

And I sat in that chair.

The moment I did so, the Clock turned green.

*

Anxiety overcame me like a tsunami, a feeling I hadn't felt before. Or maybe I had and didn't remember. Whatever it was, I felt the urge to stand, but something kept me seated. Was it the chair? Was it the Clock? Why did the Clock start a session anyway when no one was here but me?

Then, I realized. The Clock attuned to the chair. I didn't know why or how, but that was the only logical explanation. Somehow, the Clock knew when a soul needed to be in this chair, when they needed guidance. That's why it turned yellow while waiting. When a soul was ready to talk, when a Crossover session began, it turned green. Somehow, the Clock knew when the session was almost over. Either based on the way the spirit felt or when they had nothing left to talk about. Or maybe it was them coming to terms with their death or figuring out their peace.

I rubbed my face with my hands and groaned. Why did I suddenly feel exhausted? I had work to do. I couldn't sit here pondering how the Clock and the Crossover Room worked.

About to stand, a glittering shape took form on the other side of the table. My chair.

Nothing about this was right. I was now on the wrong side of the table. A soul appeared before me at the table when they were supposed to come through the arch under the Clock. They weren't supposed to arrive after the Clock turned green. Did I break the Clock? Did I shatter something in the Afterlife? Did I mess up?

Panicked, I tried to stand when the shape finished forming, giving me pause. Mouth dry, eyes wide, I slowly sat again in shock.

Me. It was me. I sat at the other end of the table. I was sitting in my chair.

How could I be on both sides of the table? I gripped my cloak with both hands, wondering if I was real. I didn't feel like I was in two places at once. Was this the end for me? Was a new Grim Reaper replacing me?

Too many emotions hit me at once. Relief at first, then worry. Fear. Confusion. Grief.

How could this be happening? Did I do something wrong?

Or was I getting some help to manage all the spirits? But there couldn't be two Grim Reapers ... could there?

Maybe there could. After all, they looked just like me. They had the same cloak, their face covered by the over-sized hood. They didn't have a scythe though, so maybe that meant they were replacing me. But I didn't want them to take my scythe. It liked it. It was mine.

Was I meant to train this Grim Reaper before they took over for me? But who were they? And why now?

I glanced at the Clock, silently cursing it. I didn't know what it had planned, but I didn't like it. Maybe it wasn't attuned to the chair and that it was my internal clock. It reached zero. Then again, I was dead already. I didn't have an internal clock. So, that was impossible.

Groaning, I buried my head in my hands. It wasn't like me to overthink. I never got carried away with my thoughts, nor did I ever worry this much. What was happening to me?

"Why did you bring me here?"

I snapped my head up to face this look-alike Grim Reaper. Their voice was mature and smooth. It was calm, though not in a reassuring sort of way.

"Excuse me?" I managed to squeak.

They leaned back in their chair, folding their arms. "Why am I here?"

How was I supposed to know?

"Come on, you must know something."

I didn't.

"Hello?" their tone changed from neutral to annoyed. They waved a hand in front of my face, and all I could do was blink in response.

So, I wasn't looking in a mirror. This Grim Reaper wasn't me. They were someone else entirely.

They threw their head back, groaning loudly. "I never thought I'd ever be back here and yet, here I am with a defective Grim Reaper."

Taken aback, I gasped. "Defective?"

I could see their teeth as they smirked from under their hood. "Ah, so you can speak and understand me. That's a start."

I glared at them. "I'm not defective and you're rude. How did you get here?"

They shrugged. "You brought me here."

"I did no such thing," I deflected. "You aren't the latest spirit I brought back from the Living World, and this isn't a typical Crossover session. So, how did you get here?"

"You. Brought. Me."

I gritted my teeth, trying to remain calm. Their demeanor changed after a moment. No longer snarky, but curious, they tilted their head to the side.

"You don't realize what you've done." It wasn't a question.

"I didn't do anything," I replied, my tone cautious.

They pointed to me. "You sat on that side of the table."

"So?"

"So, that's what brought me here."

Just as I was about to protest, I thought about thinking before speaking. The chair I currently sat in was the one spirits used to seek guidance from me. The other chair, my chair, was for the Grim Reaper to sit and guide those who needed it. By sitting on this side of the table, I triggered something. I wasn't sure exactly what, but I definitely messed something up.

I turned to the Clock. When it was yellow, it wasn't telling me a soul waited for guidance. It was telling me I needed the guidance. The Clock somehow knew. The problem was, I didn't know what I needed guidance in.

"Hello?" the other Grim Reaper reached over the table, snapping their bony fingers in my face. "If you're going to disrupt my day and force me back to this unsettling place, the least you could do is actually talk to me."

"Force you back?" I echoed. "Unsettling place?"

They rolled their head around before settling their gaze back on me. "Honestly, is that all you know how to do? Parrot?"

I narrowed my eyes at them. They weren't exactly kind. Why, of all the spirits, did I need to get guidance from this one?

"Are you going to talk to me, or what?"

"I didn't know sitting here would summon you," I stated.

"Then, why'd you sit there?" they asked, not accusingly.

"Curiosity, I guess," I answered. I couldn't admit it was because I thought the Clock was broken. They already thought I was dim; I didn't need to give them any more reason to think more unflattering things about me.

"You don't know how things work here, do you?" they sneered.

"I do, too!" I quickly retreated into myself, realizing how much I sounded like a child.

"Obviously not." They sounded like a teasing older sibling. "If you did, then you wouldn't have sat in that seat. Unless, of course, you needed to talk to me about something."

"Talk to you?" Why in the universe would I want to talk to them?

"Yes, Parrot. I'm here now, so what is it you want to talk about?"

Confusion clouded my ability to comment on the name calling. Was there something I wanted to talk about? I didn't understand how a chair and the Clock could have such power together, but then again ...

I stared at the Clock, warranting a sigh of annoyance from across the table.

"The Clock won't turn until we talk things out. We're in a Crossover session, don't you get that? The Clock only ends the session when the soul feels better or the spirit ends it themselves," they explained.

My head snapped back to them. "When the *soul* ends the session?"

"*Please* stop repeating everything I say. It's so annoying."

"Sorry," I said, shifting my weight. "I always thought the Clock ended the session when the spirit had a better understanding of their situation."

My look-a-like nodded. "Yes, but it'll also render a session short if the spirit no longer is in the right head space to talk.

That certainly explained why some sessions in the past had ended so abruptly. The Clock wasn't attuned to the chair. How silly of me to think that. The Clock was attuned to whoever sat in the chair—the spirit.

And right now, that spirit was me.

"So," they spoke again, their tone filled with frustration, "I ask *again*. Why did you bring me here?"

I held up a hand. "I'm sorry, but I need more information about what's going on."

They groaned.

"Why is the Clock attuned to me right now? I'm the Grim Reaper."

"You obviously have something bothering you that needs to get off your chest. So, what is it?"

How did I get here? Why was I the Grim Reaper? How did I become the Grim Reaper, or was I always this way? If so, how come I never got a chance to be alive in the Living World? If not, then why am I stuck as the Grim Reaper?

I stared at them, trying to quiet the voices in my head. "Why are you here?" I asked again.

They slapped their palm to their forehead. "Do you ever listen, Parrot?"

"My name isn't Parrot."

"I just explained—"

"Why *you?* Who are you? I thought I was the only Grim Reaper."

I saw their shoulders relax as they understand my question. Calmly, they answered. "There is only one at a time, but there are many Grim Reapers. I was the Grim Reaper before you."

My mouth dropped open. "How does that work?"

"I don't know if I can answer that," they said in a thoughtful tone. "It's something all Grim Reapers need to figure out on their own."

"How am I supposed to figure that out when I'm constantly helping everyone else? I never have a spare moment to myself."

"Maybe this is your way of figuring it out. Reaching out to me, I mean."

"I don't know how I reached out to you in the first place," I stated, leaving out the fact that they won't actually answer my question.

"You're a soul in need of guidance. The Grim Reaper provides guidance. You can't very well guide yourself, can you? That's where I come in."

"I didn't know this was possible," I murmured.

"Neither did I," they grunted. "But it's the only logical explanation, so, what do you want to know?"

It wasn't typical for the Grim Reaper to need guidance. Ironically, the other spirits helped me. By helping them with their issues, it allowed me to understand the Living World, the Spirit World, and myself a bit more. Although, now I felt as though I didn't know much at all.

I lifted my gaze to meet theirs, determined, "I want to know everything."

*

"*Everything* is a broad subject, Parrot. Mind narrowing it down a bit?"

I paced the room, not looking at the previous Grim Reaper, too deep in thought to pay much attention to their sarcasm.

I finally settled on what to say. "I want to know how you know everything."

"I was the Grim Reaper before you."

"That's not good enough. I'm the Grim Reaper now, and I don't know everything."

"Maybe you're too narrow-minded."

I stopped pacing, glaring at them. "What's that supposed to mean?"

They waved their hand dismissively. "You're too focused on the other spirits that you've probably never thought about how you can get out of here."

"Get out of ... the Afterlife?" I questioned, confused.

"Yes, Parrot."

"How can I leave the Spirit World? I'm the Grim Reaper."

"So was I."

So, it was possible.

I pressed a hand to my head. "One thing at a time," I said, trying to organize my thoughts. "I'm focused on the other spirits because I'm supposed to help them."

"And you do a great job of that."

Wow, I think that was a genuine compliment from them.

They spoke more when I didn't answer. "You've changed the way the Afterlife works in ways I never could. I don't think any Grim Reaper has thought of putting multiple souls together in the Crossover Room. You figured out a way to bring souls together even in death, even though they won't remember each other when they go back to the Living World." They leaned back in their chair, folding their hands behind their head comfortably. "You've made life easier for them in death. The turnaround rate of spirits heading back to the Living World is much sooner than it's ever been."

"And that's a good thing?"

"I suppose," they said with a slight shrug. "The Living World and Spirit World can't exist without the other. That's a mystery of the universe even I don't know the answer to. But if we knew all the answers—"

"There'd be no point in living," I completed.

They smirked. "Right."

"How do you remember all this? How do you know the turnaround rate of souls heading back to the Living World?" I questioned.

"My subconscious, I guess. When I sat down in this chair, it's like all this knowledge popped back into my head. Being the Grim Reaper isn't something one could easily forget, no matter how long you've been away from the title. Although, it's not like I remember it in my waking life."

"Your waking life?"

"I'm alive, Parrot," they mocked. "I'm sleeping right now. When I wake, this conversation will feel like a weird dream. I may not remember it, but if I do, I'll probably assume it was the spicy sushi I ate before bed."

I rushed back to the table, sitting down. "Wait, you're in the Living World right now? You have a physical form?"

"For now," they said. "When my internal clock runs out, I'll meet you right back here. But I'll be sitting there and you'll be sitting here." They pointed with an index finger between the two chairs.

"You mean your spirit will turn to me for guidance when you move on?" I clarified.

"Probably."

"Have we met before?"

"We have."

"When?"

"I don't remember."

"How many times?"

"Too many times to count."

"Too many ..." my voice faded away as I wondered just how long I've been the Grim Reaper for.

"Yes, Parrot," they groaned.

"Does your soul remember your time as the Grim Reaper whenever you come here?" I asked eagerly.

They shrugged again, looking around the empty space. "Not necessarily. It may look familiar to me, but that's all. No matter how many times I live and die and live again, my soul doesn't remember the Afterlife. Not completely, anyway. It's similar to how a spirit forgets their previous life over time."

"You mean how a spirit dies, grieves their previous life, and then goes back in a new physical form when they're ready to start again?"

They nodded. "It's the circle of life. Every soul learns some lessons, has experiences, makes memories, and then carries it all with them to the Afterlife. They rest and reminisce before heading back to the Living World to start all over again. Their new physical form carries those lessons into the Living World, though they don't fully remember. They have no idea they'll make a profound impact on the world, for better or worse, when they reincarnate over and over again."

"Then," I added, "when that life ends, they come back to the Spirit World as if they've never been here before."

"I don't think that's necessarily it, though I can't prove it."

"Do explain."

"Well," they began, resting their hands on the table's surface, "you know how you meet some spirits who are already at peace with their death? I think those are the souls who, deep down, remember the Afterlife. They don't realize it, but something tells them the Afterlife is nothing to be afraid of."

"That would explain a lot," I agreed.

"Those are the souls you need to look out for."

I cocked my head in confusion. Understanding my body language, they elaborated.

"Keep an eye out for the spirits who are happy to be here. They're the ones who are curious about this place, and they're also the ones already at peace or close to it upon arriving here. Have you ever had a Crossover session or two where the soul recounted happy memories from their time in the Living World? They weren't afraid at all, they had no questions about what happened to them? They were just thankful they got to live?"

I nodded.

"Those are the souls I'm talking about. They don't have regrets. They already have a deep understanding of life and death and how they work together, even if they don't realize it."

"You mean for me to keep an eye out for them so I can invite them to more group sessions?" I didn't understand what this Grim Reaper wanted.

They rolled their eyes in response. "No, don't you want to get out of here?"

"Out of ..."

"The Afterlife, Parrot."

In the midst of our conversation, I already forgot that was an option. I had never considered it before. Was that because I didn't think it was a possibility, or was it because I didn't feel the need to leave the Afterlife? Yet, the Grim Reaper sitting before me was proof it was possible. Proof that maybe cycling through Grim Reapers was part of that circle of life they mentioned. Not every soul was meant to help others on the other side, but maybe, for some, they were meant to be the Grim Reaper. Was I holding them back? Was I being selfish by staying as the Grim Reaper? I didn't do it on purpose, though. I didn't know.

Had I unknowingly caused myself, my soul, to get stuck in the Afterlife? I could move on?

"In my opinion," the Grim Reaper broke me out of my thought with a gentle tone. "Those souls, the ones who seem to have it all figured out, are the best candidates to be the next Grim Reaper."

My jaw fell open. The *next* Grim Reaper?

It made sense, of course. Obviously, I wasn't the first Grim Reaper, nor would I be the last. If they were the previous Grim Reaper, that meant I took their place. Someone would have to take mine.

I leaned forward on the table. Quietly, as though we were swapping secrets, I asked, "How exactly did I become the Grim Reaper after you?"

"I chose you," they answered bluntly.

"But what does that mean?" I pressed.

"I don't remember the process," they said, shaking their head. "But it means I was released from the Afterlife, and you got ..."

"Stuck here?"

They chuckled. "Well, it sounds cruel when you say it like that."

Cruel? Was that the best way to describe being the Grim Reaper? How could helping other souls be a bad thing?

"Didn't you like being the Grim Reaper?" I inquired.

There was a moment of silence as they stared at me in shock. Then, within a blink, they threw their head back and laughed. *"Like* being the Grim Reaper? That's hilarious! What's there to like about it?"

Rendered speechless, I couldn't think of an answer. I knew they were wrong, but I suddenly felt intimidated by their boisterous demeanor.

"Listen," they said sternly, "being in the Afterlife might as well be a prison sentence. Or, hell, as those in the Living World would believe. There's nothing here. It's dark and empty and depressing."

My gaze shifted to the colorful rose dividing the two of us.

"Nothing will change that." They snapped their fingers, and the rose vanished. "Why is it that the in-between of life and death has to be so bleak? What do we do in our physical forms to deserve coming to such a dank place? There's nothing for anyone here. It's merely an area to twiddle our thumbs until our soul feels better enough to head back to the Living World."

I frowned as the rose disappeared, wanting to fight back, but couldn't find my will to speak, not that they gave me a chance to.

"The Spirit World is nothing more than a place for us to remember all the good things we had in our previous lives that we'll never get to interact with again. Families who loved us are now gone. Our friends no longer exist. How can we love someone or something so much just to forget about it in the end? And when you're the Grim Reaper, you know more than anyone else. You know you're erasing the previous lives of millions of souls, and for what? What's the point?"

If I had an answer, I was sure I'd speak up. But nothing came to mind. They had a point. As the Grim Reaper, I didn't kill anyone, but I also didn't give the souls a chance to linger longer in the Living World. By bringing them here, did I speed up the process of them forgetting everything they once held dear? I might as well have been death like everyone in the Living World depicted.

I knew why we didn't know the answers to everything. But why bother living to chase answers you'll never get to know? You'll never get to understand?

The previous Grim Reaper lowered their tone. "When I wake up, I won't remember any of this. As angry as I am that I can't remember my previous lives, that I can't be with past friends and families, I'll be glad to wake up in the morning and believe this conversation was a wild dream. To not remember that I ever existed once before, twice before, thousands of times before who I am now is a gift. Because to remember is pain. It's a curse, just like being the Grim Reaper is."

Quietly, I tried to protest. "Being the Grim Reaper ..."

"Is. A. Curse," they spit the words. "All you do is help others, but who is going to help you, huh?"

"I don't need help," I stated firmly, finally finding my voice.

They snorted out a laugh. "Clearly! Why else would you sit in that chair? Why else would you call me here? Why else would that Clock be green?" they stretched out an arm to point at the looming green light glaring down at us.

I swallowed a lump in my throat, embarrassed. I forgot the Clock had attuned to me during this session. I didn't know why it wouldn't turn, despite still being confused. I didn't think this conversation helped, though. Sure, the Grim Reaper shed light on some things, but did they have to be so nasty about it?

Finally, the Grim Reaper calmed themself down and began speaking to me like an equal once more. "Do yourself a favor, will you? Pick a soul who's eager enough to be the next Grim Reaper. Pick someone who is already at peace, someone who is unafraid of the Afterlife. Maybe pick someone who was a good person when they were alive. Pick anyone, for all I care. But pick *someone* so you can move on with your life."

"Move on with my life," I repeated thoughtfully. "I had a life before?"

They nodded. "How do you think you got to the Afterlife in the first place?"

Everyone started here. I just assumed, over time, that I was always here. I didn't remember anything. Why couldn't I? How I got here, who I was, how many lives ... I paused my thoughts.

"How long have I been the Grim Reaper?" I stammered.

They relaxed their shoulders. "Many lifetimes."

"How many?"

"How should I know?"

"But you were the Grim Reaper before me. How many lives have you lived since then?"

"Far too many to count."

Wincing, I suggested a number. "Like a handful?"

The Grim Reaper chuckled. "Oh, no, I'd say a couple hundred at least."

For the first time, I felt the floor shift underneath me. The Clock's shine made my eyes squint, even with my hood shielding my face. I could feel the truth emitting from the Grim Reaper. There wasn't any hesitation, nor was there any remorse that they had moved on hundreds of years ago. Could they have been wrong? Maybe, but I didn't think so.

I remained the Grim Reaper all this time, taking their place so they could live.

"Can I ask you another question?" I asked, feeling like I was in a trance.

"What?" they groaned.

"You picked me, correct?"

They nodded.

"Why? Why me, of all the other spirits you spoke to?"

Then, like a punch to the gut, they answered simply, "You were enthusiastic, and I was desperate."

*

How many lives had I lived? Those memories were so far out of reach. Were they memories I wanted to forget? Is that why I had been eager to be in the Afterlife? So fascinated with this place? It was possible I wanted an extended break from the Living World and this Grim Reaper chose me to stay.

But for how long?

I couldn't imagine my previous life causing me to never want to return to the Living World. Was it possible the experiences in the Living World could leave a soul scarred? I had seen my fair share of tortured souls come through the Crossover Room. I've seen the regret, dealt with the sadness, deflected the anger, and yet … there was so much more than that.

I had met so many amazing spirits who loved life. Most of them wished for more time in the Living World. But once they joined the Afterlife, they'd soon accept their fate. They wouldn't know it, but their soul would find its way back to the Living World. They'd get to try again. They'd test out a new physical form, find more to love, experience new things, and make fresh memories.

That should be a reassuring thought. No matter how much you disliked your previous life, you'll be able to go back and try again. Right any wrongs, try new things, meet new people. But that's not how the universe works. We're not supposed to remember. We're not supposed to carry thousands of lives in our heads.

I watched the Grim Reaper from across the table. They slouched in their chair, head lolled to the side with their eyes closed, arms crossed. I knew they weren't actually sleeping. Just bored, waiting for me to sort through my endless thoughts.

If one remembered all their previous lives, they'd be just as tortured as this Grim Reaper. They didn't remember their past lives either, not in the Living World. And then their internal clock ticks down, they'll come back to the Spirit World, only remembering fragments of the life they just lived.

Yet, in this moment, deep down, as the Grim Reaper, they remember everything. It all came back to them the moment the cloak was put on them again. The moment they sat in that chair against their will.

I could understand why they felt being the Grim Reaper was a curse. It truly sounded like a burden.

Deep down, did I remember my previous lives? Was I math whiz in one life and struggled with it in the next? Was a loner, or did I surround myself with close friends? What sort of jobs had I done? I had thousands of lives living deep in my subconscious. That knowledge, whether I remember it or not, is what helps me aid all the other souls. Is it why I'm the type of Grim Reaper I am?

Who was I before? Who could I become after?

I pitied the previous Grim Reaper who so desperately wanted to forget, while I ached to remember. Then again, I was sure they pitied me for the opposite reasons.

But is it worth pitying those who are able to help others? Is it worth envying those who have what you desire? I snickered to myself. It seemed the Afterlife had similar issues with morals as those did in the Living World. We were all spirits. We just lived more simply in the Afterlife.

"Can I go home now?"

"Not yet," I replied simply, noticing them eyeing me. They groaned at my response, but remained quiet otherwise. The Clock was still green. If we measured time here like the Living World did, I was sure we'd been here for hours.

I stood and started pacing the room. Even as the Grim Reaper, it was difficult to know how the universe worked. I didn't know all of life's secrets, but it was clear now that we all knew more than we thought. More than we remembered. Before me, before this other Grim Reaper, how many Grim Reapers have there been? Millions? Has every soul had a chance to be the Grim Reaper at one point or anyone? How long has this been going on?

Why did the Grim Reaper exist at all?

I shook my head. I shouldn't be questioning why the universe works the way it does, nor should I wonder about its age. The universe worked in strange ways, so I imagined there was a purpose to the Grim Reaper. The truth was, I was no different from any of the other souls I met.

Sure, I wore a black cloak that hid my face. Yes, I could transport myself to anywhere at any time in the Living World. I could carry souls from the Living World to the Spirit World with ease. Why I was the only spirit to have this ability was beyond me.

"What was I so eager about?" I questioned, breaking the silence in the room. I stopped pacing to face the Grim Reaper.

They responded with a nonchalant shrug. "You liked this place. You thought it was cool. Totally unafraid. I thought you wouldn't mind staying here for an eternity ... or, well, until you chose a new Grim Reaper."

"Did I ask to stay here forever?"

"No. No one ever *asks* to stay here."

"But—"

"Have you ever had a soul ask if they could remain in the Afterlife? A soul who didn't want to live another life?"

Yes, I had. The spirits didn't use those words exactly, but none of them were wise to reincarnation. They all assumed they were in the Spirit World to stay. No one knew the Afterlife was another opportunity to learn more about life. All the souls who arrived here thought it was the end, not realizing they had simply gone back to the beginning.

"So many spirits are terrified of this place," the Grim Reaper continued when I didn't answer. "You were different. You found comfort here. I thought you'd be a good fit."

I narrowed my eyes. "But you said you were desperate. I get the feeling you weren't thinking about my being a good fit to lead other spirits. You didn't think of their well-being. You thought of your own, seeing an easy target and a way to get yourself out of here."

"Yes." They didn't bother denying it.

"Why would you do that?"

"Why wouldn't I?"

I made my way back to the table, knowing this conversation would go in circles. It wasn't worth it trying to understand their motives. I sat at the table again. "How did you know what to do to get out of here?"

Their lips flat-lined, as though they genuinely wished they could tell me. "I can't say. You know the rules. Souls need to figure these things out for themselves."

"But you told me how to get out of here," I countered.

"This conversation never would have ended otherwise. Besides, most of the time, we already know the answer. We just don't realize it." They winked at me.

Was that a hint? That was a lousy hint.

Though I didn't doubt it. I assumed I did know the answer. I simply forgot over time, too wrapped up in being the Grim Reaper. Or maybe I thought being the Grim Reaper was the end of the end. Maybe I've held onto the title of being the Grim Reaper for so long because I was afraid of what would come after. However, this Grim Reaper moved on to another life. The cycle continued. Being the Grim Reaper was merely a pit stop.

I was supposed to move on a long time ago and I forgot.

"Finally!"

I jumped at the Grim Reaper's exclamation. Before I could ask anything, I noticed the Clock had turned orange.

Why did it do that? I still had so many questions. We couldn't end the session here.

"I can't wait to wake up in my own bed and forget this ever happened!" The Grim Reaper stretched their arms out.

They bothered me, but I didn't want them to go. I finally had someone who understood what it was like to be the Grim Reaper. Someone who understood my role in the universe. They understood me. I didn't want to be left alone.

I had been the Grim Reaper for so long, always being there for countless spirits, always repeating the same advice, reciting the same rules of the universe over and over. I didn't know I too could reach out for guidance. I had set up group sessions for departed souls to learn from another, to support each other. What about a Grim Reaper group, huh? How come I had to do this on my own?

"Whatever questions you have will get answered. Or maybe not," the Grim Reaper said, standing from the table.

I glared at them. "Thanks for the pep talk."

They sighed. "Listen to the Clock," they said almost sincerely now. "It knows you have a better idea of what you need to do. Even if you don't realize it, you know. Otherwise, it wouldn't have turned. Trust yourself."

Trust me. I did trust myself. Didn't I?

"Will I ever see you again?" I asked.

They blinked at me, and I couldn't tell if they were touched by the question. "I hope not," came the blunt reply.

I shook my head at their snark. Trust myself. I wouldn't have made it this far if I didn't trust myself. But now I'm questioning everything.

"Choose a soul and live your life again," they reminded.

Is that what I wanted? I'll admit, it sounded ideal. I couldn't remember the last time I danced in the rain or felt the sun's warm rays. I didn't know what it felt like to be sad and comforted by a loved one. I wanted to remember what it felt like to get into a fight with someone and the satisfaction of making up with them.

I imagine myself driving a car, feeling the wind in my hair. Or maybe I'll be bald. I imagine getting good grades in school, having a job. I'd have a family to care for. Maybe find a life partner and have children.

"Live my life again ..." I repeated with a small smile.

The Clock turned red. The Grim Reaper smiled as they vanished from the room, destined to wake up and think this was a silly dream.

Now that I was alone again, I thought about the possibilities of my previous lives. I'll never remember them, but it was oddly comforting to know that, at some point, I had people who loved me. I had memories. Once upon a time, I was happy.

I waved my hand to make the single rose appear on the table again. I didn't care what the other Grim Reaper thought about this place. Even if the Afterlife was a pit stop, I'd make the most of my time here and create a welcoming environment as best as I can for the spirits.

The rose was blue again. Not red or yellow or rainbow. When I first created it, I chose the color to radiate calm at the table. Now knowing what my subconscious already knew, I wonder if I truly had calm in mind for the spirits.

I had meant to bring the rainbow petals back, but seeing the blue rose again made me realize the distance I felt from the Living World. How much I yearned to be alive again. The grief that ached inside me for all the lives I never got to live.

Group Four

IF YOU WERE GOING to die, being at home was probably the best place to do it. Familiarity would surround you, comforting you in your last moments. No machines beeping, IVs poking you, or nurses interrupting your sleep every hour.

Not that being at home makes dying any easier, of course. When souls moved on from their home, they'd hope to stay there forever. But nothing lasts forever.

Even if the souls didn't go back to the Afterlife with me and chose to stay behind, their home would change, over time. Time kept ticking in the Living World. People kept living. Houses changed or were sold to strangers.

It was common. One spirit visited me in the Crossover Room, devastated that their partner had sold their house. The one they bought and decorated together. The people who bought it torn it down to build from scratch. Everyone grieves differently.

Now I had arrived at a house to pick up a departed soul. I watched them from a corner of the room as they slowly moved across the floor, trying to touch every object in her path. She murmured words I couldn't quite make out. Afraid to disturb her process, I waited in silence.

She spent a moment with each object before moving onto the next. First, the couch. Then the coffee table, and the stack of magazines on the table. The TV. The TV remote.

I tuned into voices coming from the other room. Curiously, I poked my head into the adjacent room, which seemed to be a study of some sorts. That's when I found this soul's used physical form. It lay on the couch in the study, with two people, still alive, mourning. One was on the phone while the other sobbed.

"Goodbye ... goodbye ... I'll miss you ... I'll remember what you looked like ..."

I looked over my shoulder to see the spirit now staring at pictures on the wall. She said her goodbyes to every item, speaking to the people in the photos as though they were in the room with us. I recognized one of the men in the pictures as the man on the phone in the study. Why she said goodbye to his picture and not to him, I didn't know.

It was as though she were in some sort of trance. She knew she was dead, but couldn't—or wouldn't—believe it. Unfortunately, saying goodbye to everything wouldn't make things better. It wouldn't change anything, and it certainly wouldn't help her move on any faster.

The two people in the study made their way into the living room. I stepped out of the way, but not quickly enough for the man to feel a chill. He craned his neck to look at the ceiling vent before steering the crying woman over to the couch. He muttered something comforting to her as he helped her sit down.

"Goodbye ... I'll miss you ... you were a fun puzzle book ..."

It was then I noticed the spirit eyeing her loved ones from the other side of the room, but remained focused on objects. She was torturing herself, saying goodbye to things that didn't matter because she didn't want to believe any of it.

Normally, I liked giving the souls a few extra minutes, but I couldn't let her continue like this. I walked up to her, stretching out my hand. "It's time to go," I said gently.

She stared at me with wide eyes, glancing back and forth between me and her loved ones. Then she let out a wail and rushed over to the woman sitting on the couch. She leaped at her in an attempt to hug her.

Except she went right through the woman, thus through the couch, and onto the floor. I walked along the edge of the furniture to see her kneeling on the ground behind the couch. She held her face in her hands, crying. Before I could say any words of comfort, she turned to look at me, tears streaming down her cheeks.

"I'm not ready to let go!" she wailed.

"I know," I said softly, kneeling beside her. I held my hand out again, hoping she'd take it. "You can hold on to me instead."

She glanced back at her loved ones, and for a moment, I thought she'd try lunging at them again.

Instead, she turned her sights on me, leaping at me, wrapping her arms around in a tight hug, sobbing into my shoulder.

*

It hurt when she hugged me. I had forgotten what a hug felt like. Ever since her frigid arms wrapped around me, I craved another.

There was something satisfying about a hug. I didn't know what it was, but the feeling of holding onto someone you love so dearly is a gift. One that shouldn't be underappreciated. Because, one day, you won't be able to hug them again. It's not something that can be replicated or replaced by something else.

For me, hugging had become a distant memory, buried deep down inside me. That's why I struggled to look this spirit in the eye when she visited the Crossover Room. She didn't realize how awkward she made things for me, though it wasn't her fault.

She didn't look at me much, either. The Clock remained green on the invisible wall as we sat in silence. It was difficult for me to find anything to say to her.

After a while of sipping our beverages in silence, she finally spoke. "I never thought I'd taste tea again."

I looked up from my distant gazing to see her peering into her teacup. Did I detect a smile on her lips?

"When I died, I thought I'd never get to see or hear or do anything ever again. I thought I'd cease to exist. Just like I didn't exist before I was born."

I sipped my tea, not wanting to touch that subject.

"I don't know why I died. Why my time came so soon."

I didn't, either. It was all up to the internal clock. Even though she was relatively healthy, she ignored the pain when she went into cardiac arrest. She had been alone, so by the time someone found her, it was too late.

"When I saw my body, I kind of freaked out a little," she continued. "I didn't think I'd ever see my home again, so I wanted to remember everything about it."

I nodded, knowing she'd eventually forget anyway, but I wouldn't say anything. Bursting her bubble wasn't going to make me feel better from this funky mood I was in.

"You don't realize the little things until they're gone, you know? You don't know what you're missing until you no longer see it. How does that make sense?" she chuckled, sipping her beverage again.

"Many people take life for granted," I agreed. "Even though they know not to, it's hard to put it into practice."

"I don't think I took anything for granted," she countered.

Of course she did. Everyone did.

"I had a couch and a dog," she said, changing the subject. "He loved the couch, sleeping on it at night, and taking naps on it during the day. He was so fluffy and shed so much that no human ever sat on that couch. I kept it clean enough, but soon it became the dog's couch." She smiled at the memory, but it soon faded. "Then, he passed away. He was old, lived a good life with us. We kept the couch for a long time after that, missing his presence. It was odd, but we soon got used to his absence."

She gazed into her teacup. "Then, one day we rearranged the furniture. We finally decided it was time to get rid of that couch. No one ever sat on it, and it had been years since our dog passed. We got a new couch to replace it, even putting it in the same spot in the living room. Yet, the living room felt empty. It was the same type of couch, too. Same size, just a different color." She tore herself away from her beverage and looked at me. "How did it look so invisible? How did it feel like there was a black hole in the middle of the living room?"

I cracked a smile at the story. "Letting go of something—or someone—doesn't mean you forget. You had stared at your living room in one particular way for many years and when it changed, your brain got confused. Not in a bad way, but it remembers how things used to be and wants to go back to that time because it was safe. Comforting."

She nodded, bringing the tea to her lips. "I suppose you're right. We sometimes get so set in our ways."

"It's not easy letting go."

"No. It's not."

Back to silence. The Clock still glowed green, illuminating the room.

After some time, she spoke again. "I wasn't ready to let go of my life. The people in it or the things I did. But I wasn't ready to let go of my dog, nor his couch. I let go because I had to. It was the right thing to do. But you never know if it's actually the right choice."

"Yes, you do," I stated.

"How?"

"Your gut knows."

She sat back in her seat, grunting. "My gut's been wrong before."

"We all make choices that are right for us *at the time*," I clarified. "Life is always changing, and I don't mean rearranging furniture. Every decision you make creates a new life path for you. It's up to you whether you want to take that path or try a different route."

"What if I don't want to take either path?"

"Then backtrack. Well, you won't always be able to. Sometimes a choice is pretty set in stone, but there are times when you'll realize you may not have made the right decision. You can then back out, or do something about it to make it right."

"I supposed you're right."

I am right.

She let out a long sigh, staring out the window. "I wish I could have hugged them one last time. But I'm afraid if I did, I would have stayed like that forever."

I frowned. "You can go back, you know. Watch over them. You won't be able to hug them, but it might bring you some peace."

"Maybe," she said, deep in thought. "I think I freaked out because I can't backtrack on this path I took. I made an irreversible decision. When I felt the pain, I knew something was wrong. But I pushed it to the back of my mind. I thought if I could get through one more day, things would be fine. If I didn't think about it, maybe it would go away." She shook her head, disappointed in herself. "It's not that I wanted to die. I was in denial. I let go of my health, and because of that, my life."

The Clock turned orange, and the spirit stood from the table. She wiped a tear from her eye, though she smiled.

"I can't face my family right now. I can't bear the thought of them not forgiving me for letting go too soon."

I didn't have many words of wisdom for her in my back pocket. The Clock had turned, which signaled she was done with this conversation. Even if she got her health checked, her internal clock would have still reached zero, and she'd be here with me. I didn't know what else to say in this moment, so I let her go.

"Thank you," I said to her as she exited.

She stopped, looking over her shoulder. "For what?"

"The hug."

"Oh," she said, confused. "You're welcome."

Chaos. That was the room's atmosphere when I arrived at the hospital to pick up another soul. I stood vigil in the corner, watching the scene unfold.

"You have to do something! It's not her time!"

"We did all we could. I'm so sorry."

"Honey ..."

"He said he would fix her!"

A mother begging. A doctor trying to stay professional and impartial. A father trying to be strong for his wife. It was a moment that was never easy to witness.

"What's going on?"

The high-pitched voice came from beside me, but when I looked to my right, no one was there. I looked further down to see a child standing, watching her parents with curiosity.

"Did I die? Is that why Mommy is so sad?" she asked.

I drew in a sharp breath. "Yes."

The young girl watched as her mother pulled away from her father, throwing herself on top of her daughter's corpse. She wailed, and her husband stood beside her, rubbing his wife's back while crying softly. With his other hand, he picked up his daughter's small hand, rubbing the back of it with his thumb. The doctor quietly dismissed himself, as did the nurse, after she turned off the monitors.

"We can go now, if you'd like," I offered. I was sure it was tough for her to see her parents in such a state, not that anyone could blame them.

"In a minute," she said, observing her parents. "Why are they so loud?"

I hesitated, trying to find the right words. "They're telling the world how much they love you."

"Oh." She stepped away from me, walking closer to her mother and father.

She placed a hand on the small of her father's back, as that's all she could reach. Her other hand landed on her mother's hand, even though she couldn't hold it. She leaned forward in between her parents.

"I love you, too," she whispered.

Instantly, as if she had heard her daughter's voice, the mother stopped sobbing, though still hugging her daughter's lifeless body, as an eerie calm enveloped the room.

*

The child entered the Crossover Room with a skip in her step. She sat down at the table, her legs dangling. She swung them in the air, content. I had offered her hot chocolate, and she drank it with a smile on her face.

As painful as it was, it wasn't uncommon for a young child to move on to the Afterlife. I didn't know why the internal clock kept their time in the Living World so short compared to others. Despite that, it was rare they visited me in the Crossover Room.

Kids were innocent. They were born that way, not learning otherwise until much later in life. They often didn't have regrets. Children didn't have the same worries as adults. It was easy for them to make friends and they accepted everyone.

Spirits came to the Crossover Room to speak about their deaths. What happened to them, what they left behind, what they should do next ... kids didn't pay attention to any of that. They spent their time in the Living World carefree and, in the Spirit World, they were eager to explore. It was a new adventure for them.

"Do you have more?" she asked, putting her empty mug on the table.

"Of course," I said, refilling it.

She took the mug again, using both hands, and drank. She giggled. "Mom and Dad wouldn't let me have this much chocolate. They always said I'd get a sugar rush and wouldn't be able to sleep. Now I can have as much as I want because I'm dead!"

I nearly choked on my cocoa as she spoke.

"It's like when you're sick," she said. "You can eat all the ice cream you want."

I watched her drink more hot chocolate. She had been sick for a long time, so I knew she spoke from experience.

She frowned at her mug, putting it on the table. I was about to ask if she already needed another refill, but then noticed it was still half full.

"Is something wrong?" I asked.

She looked at me with curiosity in her gaze. "Why were Mom and Dad so sad?"

I shifted my weight in my seat. "I think because they'll miss you."

"But I'm still here."

"Well ... yes, but not in the same way you once were."

"Because I'm dead?"

"Right. You can visit them, but they won't be able to hear or see you, I'm afraid."

She nodded. "I think they heard me before we came here."

"Yes, it almost seemed like they did," I replied thoughtfully. It was something I'd never seen before. Maybe it was because since she had just moved on, she still had a good connection to the Living World? Or maybe it was simply the power of youth.

"I don't get why they were so sad, though," she continued. "Mommy told me I could help other kids."

"We all have the ability to help others," I agreed.

"No," she shook her head, "if I died."

"What do you mean?"

"Something about giving my insides to them."

"An organ donor," I clarified, understanding what she meant.

"I think so," she agreed. "Mommy and Daddy asked me a few days ago if that's something I wanted to do. They said if something happened to me, other kids could have my insides."

"Yes, since you're not in your physical form anymore—since you're not alive," I tried to explain it simply to her, "the doctors can take your organs and transplant them to kids who may need them."

"Transplant?"

"Your organs might be stronger than theirs. So, they'd take yours and be able to live longer."

"My mom said it would help kids stay alive longer," she nodded. "That's why I agreed to do it."

"That's very kind of you."

It sounded to me as though they knew their daughter wouldn't be going home. I found it endearing that they asked her permission before she moved on, explaining it to her. I didn't know the extent of her illness, but it sounded like they did all they could.

"So, why were they so sad?" she asked again.

I shook my head. "I'm not sure I understand the answer you're looking for. Your parents love you and know they won't be able to see you again for a long time. Their sadness was their way of grieving for you, expressing how much they'll miss you and love you."

"Why didn't they just say so?"

"I'm sure they did."

"All I heard was Mom crying."

"Well ... yeah, but I'm sure she's told you many times before how much she loves you."

"She has." That made her smile.

I grinned, too. "At that moment, crying was the only way she knew how to express her feelings."

"By being sad?"

I nodded. "Sometimes sadness can mean happiness. Have you ever been so happy you cried?"

She thought about it for a moment and then perked up. "I cried when I got a new bike for my birthday once!"

"See, it's just like that."

"Mom's happy I died?"

Wait, no. That's not what I meant. "Sadness can also mean love. When you miss someone so much that it makes you sad, it means you love them very much."

The young girl let her gaze wander in thought. Then she rested her elbows on the table, looking at me. "I think I get it. Mom and Dad love me so much that they'll miss me and cry about it. But I don't want them to be sad. I want them to be happy. It's a good thing I died, right?"

My mouth gaped open, unsure how to navigate this conversation.

"I mean," she continued, "if I didn't die, then my organs wouldn't get donated. I'd need them, right?"

"Right," I replied, lingering on the word.

"I died so others could live."

Speechless. That's what I was. I didn't understand how, but children were the wisest of us all. If there were a bright side to her death, that would be it. She wasn't slightly bothered by her death, which was why she wasn't upset about leaving her parents. She was already at peace because she knew her purpose.

"I did a good thing ... didn't I?" she asked, her tone filled with uncertainty.

"Yes," I said, trying to keep my composure. "You did a very good thing. Many other children will get to live because of you and that's beautiful."

She grinned. "And maybe Mom and Dad will let them ride my bike when they can play again!"

I smiled. "Donating your organs *and* your toys? My, that's very a grown-up thing for you to do."

She giggled, grabbing her mug once more. "I'll get to go back again soon," she declared.

"To visit your parents?"

"To start over. I think I'll get another chance."

The Clock turned red. She politely said her thanks and skipped out of the room, leaving me shocked at how aware she was. I knew very well she'd get the chance to explore the Living World again in a new, healthy physical form. Maybe she'd even get the opportunity to meet her parents again.

I arrived in the next spirit's bedroom. They stood on the other side of the room from me, staring into a full-length mirror. She tilted her head this way and that, twisting her body around. I didn't know what she saw. Souls didn't have a reflection.

I stood behind her. "Excuse me?" I said quietly, afraid of interrupting the flow of whatever she was doing.

My words didn't startle her, and she didn't look in my direction. Her focus remained on the mirror as she asked, "Do you see anything? Anyone?"

"I only see you, but not in the mirror," I replied.

She dropped her arms by her side. "I don't see anything, either. Why?"

"You're a spirit now," I explained. "You're a transparent silhouette of your physical form."

She turned around, lazily pointing a finger at her dead body. "You mean that?"

"Yes, you." I had never heard a soul depict their former self as an object rather than a human being.

She chuckled. "Me. Sure. Honestly, the body doesn't look any different than it did when I was still inside it."

"What do you mean?"

"I was sick. Always sick. Needed to be in bed most of my life, resting. Never exerting myself. Always laying down doing nothing," she glared at her physical form. It looked peaceful in bed, like it was sleeping, but we both knew that wasn't true.

"I had so many surgeries," she whispered to me, turning her attention back to the mirror. But all we could see was her physical form lying in bed behind us. "So many scars. So many marks. But now? Now, it's all gone." She twisted her body this way and that again, straining to see something in the mirror. Something I knew she'd never see again.

*

"How were my parents?"

It was the first thing she asked when we met in the Crossover Room. I didn't have an answer for her, though. "I don't know. I came back here with you."

"You don't know what goes on when a person dies?"

"No. I wasn't there before you moved on, and I'm not there after I bring you here." I didn't have a map of the Living World. I went where I was needed, where my scythe told me to go.

"But you said I could go back if I wanted?" she questioned.

I nodded. "You'll still be a spirit, but you'll remember where your home was. Those memories are still fresh, so you can take advantage of that and visit your friends and family whenever you'd like."

She hummed before dipping a finger into her steaming tea. She didn't react to its heat, though her expression switched to wonder.

"Those memories are still fresh," she repeated, still staring into her tea, "like I'm going to forget them?"

"Eventually."

"Why?"

"It's how things work around here."

"When I forget ... what will I do then?"

"You'll make new memories."

Confusion clouded her face, but she didn't press further. Instead, she sipped her tea, and we sat in silence for what felt like forever.

She glanced at the Clock, which was still green. "I don't want to forget my parents. But if I'll forget what I put them through... no, that would only make me feel better, not them." She looked at me. "Do you want to know why I wanted to see myself in the mirror?"

"Sure," I encouraged.

"Well," she leaned back in her chair, "it's not like I *wanted* to see myself. It was actually a relief I couldn't see myself. I couldn't see the marks. They were all gone. I know they're still there, but now they're hidden."

"What marks, if you don't mind my asking?"

"Scars from my surgeries," she stated. "When I was born, I was in the NICU for quite some time. I was born too early and too sick. I survived long enough to go home, only to need surgery before my first birthday. Then another four years later. And another two years after that." She looked herself over as though she could see her body, but it was basically vapor.

"My body ..." she whispered. "It was disgusting."

I frowned, not responding. I hoped she'd continued speaking, for I didn't know what to say in this moment.

Luckily, she did. "Sometimes my mom would catch me looking at my stomach in the mirror. I have—had—a long scar right down the middle. It looked like I had been abducted by aliens and they cut me open."

She sneered at her own analogy. "Anyway, she'd see me staring at it, looking at all my scars, all the pokes and prods in my skin from needles and IVs and ... she'd get so sad. Sometimes angry. Sometimes she'd panic. I don't know what she was thinking. She's rush over to me and pull my shirt down. She'd tell me not to look. Other times she'd reassure me I was beautiful. I never knew what sort of pep talk I'd get." She shook her head. "Honestly, I think my mother was just as disgusted as I was. But as the mother, she was supposed to make me feel better. I guess she tried sometimes, but over time I think it was hard for her to stay positive."

The spirit paused to sip her tea. I stayed silent, knowing she had more to say.

"I wasn't allowed to go to pool parties. I think my mom thought people would make fun of the way my body looked. When we had company, I'd have to wear clothes that covered all my scars. I didn't have to at first, but one of my younger cousins asked about a mark on my arm once and my mom panicked. I don't know why it bothered her so much.

"I think it bothered my dad, too, but I can't be sure. He never talked about it. He simply paid the medical bills without a word. Every time I got wheeled away into surgery, the last image I'd see was of him smiling and giving me a thumbs up. I think he tried to be brave for my sake, maybe for my mother's, too. But I'm sure that as soon as I was out of sight, the smile faded while he consoled my mother, crying into his shoulder. Maybe he cried, too. They spent many hours in the waiting room, constantly wondering if I would even make it out of surgery alive."

"But you always did," I said softly.

"I did," she nodded. "But I'd emerge with another mark. Another reminder of my illness. Another token of ruining my parents' lives."

"You don't really believe that, do you?" I asked, shocked at her words.

"I do," she sneered. "My father worked three jobs to pay the hospital bills on top of the regular bills. My mother quit her job to stay home with me because I needed round-the-clock care." She looked down at her stomach again. "Even on my good days, the scars were there, but now? Now they're gone. It's as if it never happened. I'm sure my death lifted a heavy weight from my parents' shoulders."

"I don't believe that at all," I said, sterner than I meant.

Taken aback, she looked at me with wide eyes.

"In some ways, sure, your moving on might be a relief to your parents, but only because they know you're no longer sick. I doubt they're feeling relieved for their sakes. Otherwise, they wouldn't have tried so hard. They wouldn't have rearranged their lives to help you through your illness."

"I guess so, but you could argue they did that because they're my parents."

"Not everyone is so lucky to have parents who take that responsibility seriously."

She pressed her lips together, turning her gaze away.

"Do you think your parents regret having you?" I asked.

"No," she said quickly, looking at me again. "But I do wish my mother accepted me for how I was. I got the feeling she was afraid of me."

"I think she was afraid *for* you," I corrected. "What she did was her way of protecting you. Right or wrong, she did it for you. Please, don't think I'm invalidating your feelings, but I don't want you to think negatively of your parents."

She smiled at me, as though she pitied me. "I get that. I'm grateful for all my parents did for me. I only wish she could have seen how amazing my body was."

"What do you mean?" I asked.

She chuckled. "It's not pretty to look at, but it worked. I could walk, talk, see, hear. I could feel things. Physically, emotionally. I could think for myself and make decisions. Some days were hard, but I was able to leave the house, go to school, hang out with my friends. My body did a lot for me. Looks aren't everything."

I nodded, realizing she had a point. "You wanted your mother to look past the scars, past the surgeries, and see you."

"Yes," she said quietly. "Best of all, my body was strong enough to withstand all those surgeries. Why I didn't wake up that morning, I don't know." She smiled. "Twenty-five isn't a long time to live, but honestly? I'm so thankful for the time I had. And now," she stood as she the Clock turned. "My parents can have the rest of their lives."

The first to arrive was the twenty-five-year-old. Then a middle-aged woman. Finally, a young girl. I knew she didn't need another session, but I hoped she'd help the other women. When she skipped into the room, the two other souls exchanged shocked glances. No one ever assumes a child would be in the Afterlife, but it wasn't impossible. They watched in silence as the child took the middle sit in between them at the table.

"Cocoa?" I asked, and she nodded excitedly.

As soon as everyone had their drinks, the young adult looked at me. "Is there something you wanted to say to us?" She was uneasy, and I wasn't sure if it was the presence of the child or if she thought they were in trouble.

"I hoped you'd have something to say to each other," I answered. "These group sessions are to help you connect with other souls that reside in the Afterlife, to help you go forward together. If you want."

None of them spoke. The two adults looked at each other again while the girl sipped her hot chocolate.

"How's your cocoa?" I asked her with a friendly smile, trying to ease the tension.

"It tastes funny now, but still good," she answered.

"I'm glad. How have you been?"

"Good."

"Have you visited your parents at all?"

"Uh-huh."

"How are they?"

"Still sad."

"I bet. It'll take time, but they'll be okay."

"I know," she grinned at me. "They'll be so happy when the other kids get to play again because of me."

Intrigued, the young adult joined the conversation. "Were you sick, too?"

The child looked at me. "Yeah. Did you die from being sick?"

"I did."

The young girl turned to the adult. "Were you sick?"

She hesitated, but then nodded. "I was too stubborn to get it checked out, though."

"Oh," the little one replied. "My mom always says to listen to your body."

The adult snorted. "Your mom sounds wise."

"She's the smartest person I know."

"Moms tend to be very smart. Maybe I wouldn't have been so stubborn about going to the doctor if my mom were still alive. She might have helped me," the woman stated.

"Your mom died?" the child asked.

"About two years ago, yeah."

"That's sad. I wonder where she went."

The adult turned to me with a sudden realization. "Is my mom here?"

I nodded. Most spirits didn't move on to their next life until this one was complete. Even though they were dead, they still had loose ends to tie up. There were plenty of things they could still do for themselves and their loved ones.

"Why didn't she greet me when I arrived?" she asked.

"She's not the Grim Reaper," I replied bluntly. "You'll find each other."

She leaned back in her chair, grinning. It had been difficult for her to let go of the things she knew in the Living World, but all of that seemed forgotten now. Knowing she'd get to see her mom again was comforting enough, knowing she wasn't going through this alone.

"When they take my organs, will I look weird?" the child asked, completely changing the subject.

I raised a brow at her. "Weird how?"

"I don't know. How will they get my organs out of my body? Do they have to cut me open?"

I noticed the young adult in the room wince. She had been awfully quiet, not looking at anyone, though it was clear she was listening to the conversation. For now, I turned my attention back to the little one. "I'm not entirely sure how they do it, but you won't look weird. They'll know how to put you back together nicely."

Satisfied with that answer, she resumed drinking her cocoa.

I turned to the young adult. "How are you doing?"

She replied with a shrug, not facing any of us at the table.

"Are you sad?" the young girl questioned. She had an uncanny ability to act like she wasn't paying attention, only to chime in at the right moments. It was true what they said about children. They were always listening.

The other spirit shook her head. "No, I'm fine."

"You look sad."

No answer.

"What's wrong?"

The woman looked over her shoulder at the child, though she didn't look annoyed. She then turned to face the kid. "Did your mom ... well, was she ever afraid of you?"

"Of me?" the young one repeated.

"Did you have a lot of surgeries?"

"I had treatments that made me tired."

"But did you have any marks on your body?"

"I lost my hair."

The young woman nodded, looking defeated. "Right. I'm sorry you went through that."

"Me too," the little one said, putting a hand on the other's knee. "I heard surgeries are scary. Some of my friends at the hospital had to have surgeries."

"You witnessed a lot in your time in the Living World, huh?" the middle-aged woman observed.

The young girl shrugged. "I didn't see a lot. I stayed in the hospital for a long time. I couldn't go to school or to the park to play. My friends had to stop visiting me for some time, so I only saw the other sick kids. We had toys at the hospital and the nurses were fun, but I didn't see the outside much."

Both adults glanced at each other again, rendered speechless. Suddenly, their time in the Living World didn't seem so bad.

Not understanding how uncomfortable the other two were, the little girl turned to the young adult. "I saw a lot of moms scared of their kid's illness. Is that what you meant? Did you get your words confused?"

Shaking her head, the young adult replied. "No, my mom was afraid of me. I had a lot of surgeries and they made my body look weird. I don't think my mom liked it."

"She didn't like how the surgeries made you feel tired?"

"No, I think the marks on my body made her nervous."

"Oh," the young one drawled as though she understood. "Moms and dads got nervous at the hospital all the time. My mom and dad would sometimes talk to them and help them feel better. I didn't always understand, but Mom told me that sometimes it's hard for adults to be strong all the time. That's why the parents at the hospital would help each other out. She said that when they had extra strength to give, they'd share it with the other moms and dads. Maybe your mom needed someone to share their strength with her?"

The young adult shrunk in her chair. "My mom really only had my dad. He was good at putting on a brave face, but I'm sure that took a toll on him. If what you say is true, then my dad was always strong enough for the both of them. But I don't know what happened between them when I was in surgery or recovery."

Grinning, the girl hugged herself. "I bet your mom and dad hugged each other tight. They probably talked about all the things you'd get to do when you were done with surgery. Because the surgery would help, right?"

"Only for a little while."

"But it let you go outside and play?"

There was hesitation, but she finally nodded and wiped a tear away.

Not able to read the room, the girl clapped her hands together. "And even though it wouldn't last forever, they knew they had more time to spend with you and that was probably exciting for them!"

Both adults cracked smiles. It was hard not to with such enthusiasm in the room.

The adult reached over to the twenty-five-year-old. "Did your mom tell you she didn't like the way you looked?"

The young adult shook her head. "Not necessarily. But she always got nervous looking at my scars."

"We don't always know the right thing to say. Your mother hadn't gone through anything like that before and there's no parenting manual. I'm sure she didn't actually think that, but didn't know how to express her worries to you."

"We're only trying to tell you that you have nothing to worry about," I chimed in. "I fully believe your parents loved you with all their hearts, or else they wouldn't have acted as they did. I'm sorry your mother didn't always know how to show it, but I don't believe they loved you any less."

"It never bothered me, though. It bothered me because it bothered her," she said.

"Did you guys ever talk about it?" the adult asked.

After some hesitation, the young adult shook her head. "She'd tell me how beautiful I was but would also make sure my scars were covered. I could never tell how she really felt, but actions speak louder than words."

"True," the other spirit replied.

"I don't blame my mom. I know my parents loved me. But I guess I can't expect others to accept me for who I am if I can't accept myself."

"It's goes both ways. It's hard to accept yourself when others look past you."

"Exactly. It's why I'm relieved to be dead. It's all over. My parents don't have to suffer anymore. Neither do I."

The Clock turned orange, even though I felt there was still so much to discuss. Although the conversation never ended in the Crossover Room; It was merely a stepping-stone to help the souls understand what to do next. They still had work to do to understand their purpose, find their pace, and start again.

Time was made up by those in the Living World, but it was extremely important to them. Yet, they often wasted it. The child didn't need guidance, but she helped the two adults see how valuable their time was in the Living World. It was a lesson every soul needed to learn, but it was one that never came easily.

Group Five

Most of the time I needed to rip the bandage off to get the spirit to go to the Afterlife with me. Too many times the souls were in denial or too distraught. They were confused or angry. But this soul? Oh, no. This spirit danced around his hospital room with glee. I couldn't interrupt his celebration.

"Do you see me? Can you see what I'm doing?" they shouted toward me, even though the room wasn't large. I could see and hear them just fine.

"I see you," I stated like a proud parent watching a six-year-old attempt a cartwheel.

And in that moment, he did. He tried to do a cartwheel. He failed miserably at it, but at least he couldn't get hurt or knock anything over.

"I haven't been able to do that since I was a kid!" He ran around the room with his arms stretched wide as though he flew like an airplane.

He was like this when I arrived. I tore my eyes away from his childlike theatrics and watched everyone else in the room, all the people who were still alive. The man's body, only middle-aged, was surrounded by friends and family. They grieved over his body, telling stories about him to one another. I thought it was something he'd want to hear, but he paid no mind to everything else in the room.

"Do you see me jumping?" he asked. I turned my attention back to him to witness him doing jumping jacks.

"We need to leave soon," I warned.

"Aw, really?"

"Yes."

"Where are we going?" he asked, finally standing still.

"The Afterlife."

"Oh." He turned to face his family. Then he looked over his shoulder at me, pointing to his loved ones. "I'll never see them again?"

"You can visit from time to time," I answered.

He grinned. "I'll still be able to walk?"

"Of course."

"Then what are we waiting for? Let's go!"

*

Out of the millions of souls I had helped crossover, I had rarely encountered someone who was so excited to be in their spirit form. Most of the time, it was because they didn't like how their life shaped up. Other times it was because they were regretful. Or maybe a loved one had already moved on and they wanted to see them again.

This soul was different. He ran around the Crossover Room like a little kid let loose on a playground. He jumped, ran in circles, did squats, kicked his legs, and laughed the entire time. He was far too happy with his condition to care about anything else, which was nice. However, spirits didn't run out of breath. If I didn't stop him, I was afraid he'd run around the Crossover Room for all eternity.

"Let's sit down for a minute," I said loud enough to get his attention, but not stern. I stood from my seat to get a higher vantage point as I motioned to the chair across from me.

"I never want to sit again," he declined.

"Fine," I said, walking around the table. I pulled his chair out from the table and then did the same to mine. "Stand with me."

Accepting the invite, he wandered over to the table with a small pep in his step. "What's up?" he asked.

"Would you like to discuss anything?" I asked.

"About what?"

"Where you are, death ... anything."

He rolled his eyes upward, deep in thought. "No, I don't think so."

But the Clock was still green. He must have been here for a reason. Not every soul had problems they needed to talk about or questions they needed answers to. Some enjoyed talking about the highlights from their life.

"Care to share your excitement?" I prompted, pointing to his legs.

The grin on his face grew. "They work!"

"Yes, they do," I agreed.

"Sorry," he chuckled. "It's just that I haven't been able to use my legs in a long time."

"May I ask why?"

"It was an accident," he calmly explained. "When I was a teenager, I got paralyzed from the waist down." The memory didn't seem to bother him as he recounted the story, though his enthusiasm certainly subdued. "I was seventeen and had gotten my driver's license. I couldn't wait to drive myself places. I was only getting ice cream for myself and my parents. My mom was reluctant to let me go alone, but I wanted to go myself so we could celebrate together with ice cream. Something to mark my independence."

"That sounds like a wonderful idea," I encouraged, even though I knew where this story would end.

"It was," he snorted lightheartedly. "The ice cream shop was only fifteen minutes away. I got there safe and sound, but on the way home ..." he looked at me sharing a somber grin. "I pulled out of the parking lot to be met with a set of traffic lights. I had the green and so did the guy coming the opposite way. I think he dozed at the wheel or something? I don't exactly remember, but he swerved into my lane." He shifted his weight, folding his arms. "I didn't know what to do. I froze. He hit me head-on. Next thing I knew, I was waking up in the hospital, not being able to feel my legs."

"I'm sorry you had to go through that," I said.

He acknowledged my sympathies with a nod. "My mother cried over me while I lay in the hospital bed, thankful I was alive. She didn't care I wasn't able to use my legs anymore. It was the best-case scenario, I guess. According to the doctor, I mean. I think I had a concussion, too, but ultimately, it could have been way worse."

I noticed he eyed my tea, so I made a cup appear before him. He picked it up, took a sip, and held it up in thanks. Then, he continued his story. "My dad felt so guilty letting me go alone. But it wasn't his fault. It wasn't anyone's fault. It didn't matter that I was young and a new driver. An accident can happen to anyone at any time."

Intrigued by his story, I bent my knees to sit. But then I remembered my chair wasn't behind me anymore, so I stood tall again. The spirit didn't seem to notice. He kept talking.

"I was in the hospital for a bit, obviously," he said. "After a couple of days, I had another visitor. It was the other driver. He felt guilty, so he brought me flowers, apologizing profusely for hitting me and causing myself and my family so much pain. He told me he already spoke to his insurance and admitted to being completely at fault. Also, he said he'd pay for what he could. I didn't know until much later, but he had paid for half of my hospital bill."

"That was kind of him," I stated, impressed. "Admitting he was at fault to the insurance company is enough of a big deal."

"Absolutely," he agreed. "My father wanted to sue him. I didn't know about that until much later in life, too. I guess he and my mother discussed it for a while. The next time they visited me and asked where I got the flowers from, I told them the other driver came by. That same day, my parents found out he had paid for half my medical bills. It was all he could afford. The insurance called them the same day and told them they had nothing to worry about since the man confessed to being at fault." He laughed at the irony. "You see, my parents wanted to sue out of hatred and defiance. But in the end, they realized it was a genuine accident. When they saw how much the man tried to make things right, they didn't have the heart to sue him."

"I'm glad to hear that," I kindly said. Not that I was one to judge others' actions, but I always liked a story where everyone got along and there were no misunderstandings.

"My parents invited him to dinner," he told me. "He was a lonely man, older than my parents, but not old enough to be my grandfather. He didn't have any family around, so we kind of adopted him. He'd join our family for holidays and attended my high school graduation. We grew close and, over time, the accident was forgotten. My wheelchair was a clear reminder, but not of a day where I lost the use of my legs, but of a day where we made a new friend."

The Clock turned orange as he continued.

"All was forgiven through action, not words. Over time, we all healed from the accident—mentally and emotionally, not physically, of course. But now," he lifted one leg, stretching it out as far as it could go, "I can walk again! And I'm so happy."

I couldn't help but smile at his enthusiasm. The Clock turned red almost as soon as it turned orange. He had already made his peace long ago. He left the Crossover Room skipping, and I watched him proudly.

He would make a good candidate to be the next Grim Reaper. That spirit wasn't the type to take living for granted and he learned some valuable lessons in the Living World. He and his family turned a horrible situation into a positive one.

He truly knew what it meant to heal. He understood how important time was, how essential it was to forgive. I was sure losing the use of his legs was frustrating and difficult to some extent, but he never discussed it. It was as though he forgot about that part of his journey. He only remembered the good parts.

That spirit was someone who should remain in the Afterlife and help guide new souls. Then again, maybe the Living World needed his positive outlook on life.

"I knew I had a soul, but I didn't think I *was* my soul. I thought I was me and the soul made me go."

When I arrived at the next destination to pick up a new spirit, I found her standing over her dead body in the middle of a park. It was far too early in the morning, with no one else around.

She looked at me, knowing I could see her. It didn't seem to bother her, though. She seemed content having something to talk through this with.

"This laying here," she pointed to her physical form on the ground, "is just a shell. It's hollow."

I nodded. "You're not wrong. Our souls need something to take shelter in, and that's the form of a human body." Or another mammal, however you wanted to look at it. But I wasn't about to stir that pot.

"It's interesting," she declared, then looked at our surroundings. "I can't believe I forgot my phone. If I had that, I would have been able to call an ambulance for myself," she chuckled. "But I guess that's just the way things are supposed to be, huh?" She turned her head to look at me.

"Yes," I agreed. "Our time comes when we least expect it." In her case, it was a routine morning jog in the park.

"Indeed. Although, I didn't expect it to happen to me doing something I love. Every morning for four years I ran in this park. Why today? Why now did my heart decide to give out?" She wagged a finger at me and started pacing. "I knew something felt funny. I thought I was coming down with a cold. That's why I took the shortcut. I guess I was wrong."

I didn't answer. Her words were true, though I couldn't read her feelings. She seemed indifferent about death. I assumed she was confused or maybe angry at how things ended for her, but she didn't show it. She didn't bargain with me to have another chance. Her fascinated tone told me she knew more than she said. She had felt pain in her chest and ignored it.

It was something many people did. They'd be in denial about something and make light of the situation or ignored it all together, hoping it'd go away. Then something goes wrong and instant regret sets in. They'd cry about how they should have done this, and should have done that. But it'd be far too late at that point.

"What do I do now?"

I looked up from her body to see the spirit standing a few feet away from me with her hands on her hips.

"Now, I take you home," I said, extending a hand.

No questions, no hesitation. She walked closer to me and placed her hand over my cold bony fingers, and we were off to the Afterlife.

*

"This isn't what I expected the Afterlife would look like," the spirit claimed, looking around at the nothingness.

I couldn't count how many times a spirit had told me that. Ignoring the comment, I offered her a beverage. Her face lit up when I mentioned hot chocolate.

When the mug appeared in front of her, she picked it up with both hands, smelling the rim. She grinned. "Okay, this *really* isn't what I expected. If someone told me I'd get to drink hot chocolate all the time, I would have wanted to come here sooner. I don't have to worry about the sugar intake or weight ... this is great!"

I smiled at her reaction, even though she wouldn't get to drink hot chocolate whenever she wanted. "You will begin to lose your sense of taste and smell overtime," I stated.

She nodded, but didn't seem to mind my statement. "So," she put her cup down, folding her hands on the table. "What happens now?"

"You can hang around the Spirit World if you'd like, such as finding past loved ones or make new friends. Or you can head back to the Living World and visit your loved ones who are still alive," I explained.

The spirit sat taller. "Can I go back to the spot where I died?"

I nodded. "Is there a reason you want to go back there?"

"I'm wondering if anyone found my body yet. Will they think I was murdered? Get an autopsy for me? What about my funeral?"

Time in the Living World had probably moved on so much at this point, her funeral preparations were probably in motion.

"You can attend your funeral, if you want. I'm sure your body was already picked up safe and sound."

"But will they know the right people to call?"

"Of course. They'll call the authorities and—"

"That's not what I mean."

I paused.

"Will the authorities know to call my family? I forgot my phone," she clarified.

"Did you have your ID on you?"

She sheepishly looked at me, not answering.

I cracked a smile at her worry. "I wouldn't stress about it. Your physical form will make it back to the right people and you'll get a proper burial with your friends and family around."

"But how will they *know*?"

I shrugged. "There's no way to know, but I have faith in them. I can't imagine your family will assume you've been running for several hours straight. And you always ran in the same spot, correct?"

She laughed. "Actually, my husband gets nervous when I run in that spot. He usually runs with me because he doesn't like me to be alone, but he wasn't feeling well, either. He's probably going to kick himself for not being there for me. I don't want him to blame himself that I didn't make it home." Tears welled in her eyes.

I frowned. "Unfortunately, that's not something you can control. Your husband will grieve for you no matter what, and that very well might involve him blaming himself. He won't do that forever, though. That's not to say he'll get over your death quickly, but he'll find his way. He'll heal in time."

She sipped her cocoa as I spoke. "My husband did so much for me. I didn't want things to end this way. He was still sleeping when I left. I didn't even say goodbye to him. I didn't want to wake him since he wasn't feeling well. I left a note for him on the counter, at least. He'll have that to remember me by."

I refilled her mug, and she nodded her thanks. "I'm sure he'll have a lot more than a note to remember you by," I said.

She laughed. "You're right. Still, even though it wasn't out loud, he'll know I loved him. I wrote it on the note. With a little heart."

"I'm sure that made him smile when he woke up."

"Yeah," her voice faded as she thought about something else. Her gaze wandered to the window, looking out into the darkness. "Everything's hollow," she observed.

"Excuse me?"

"Us. The Afterlife. It's all empty."

I found myself following her gaze, looking out the hole in the wall that mimicked a window. There was nothing to see. I knew that, but I had a weird feeling she could see something.

"I wouldn't say it's empty," I said, defending the Spirit World. "We're all here."

"But we're empty, too." She looked at me.

"We're still beings."

"We're shells of our former selves."

I shook my head. "The physical form is the shell, if that's how you want to look at it. You are your spirit and your spirit is you. The body is just something to help you navigate the Living World better because, as souls, we don't have the same senses."

"Exactly. We're empty. Our bodies are hollow without our souls and our souls are just as hollow without a body. We can't have one without the other."

I looked down at myself as if I weren't real. She wasn't entirely wrong. The Spirit World and Living World were connected in many ways, even though they were so very different and far apart.

"True, but only to a certain extent. We're proof of this," I countered, pointing between her and me. "A soul can live without a body, but a body can't live without a soul."

It was why the physical form fell limp as soon as the spirit was pushed out of the vessel. The physical form, already used, would get buried in the ground or burned, never to be used again. Eventually, the soul would find a replacement body and begin a new life in the Living World.

"But zero plus zero still equals zero," she remarked.

I tilted my head in confusion. "I'm sorry, I don't follow."

She shifted in her chair, leaning closer. "You say that we can live without a body but not the other way around, but both are empty without the other. So, no, you can't have one without the other. Because without a body, the soul is nothing. And without a soul, the body is nothing. Zero plus zero is zero. If you add a soul to a body, then you have something—a living being."

"I suppose," I replied, following her logic. "But we're still alive, regardless. The soul *is* the living being, with or without a physical form."

"Is it, though?"

I opened my mouth but hesitated to speak. Instinctively, I wanted to stand my ground. However, I couldn't help but realize she brought up some decent points, and I didn't know how I could defend my logic against hers.

"You said before I wouldn't have my senses. Our senses are part of what helps us live."

"But not everyone has all their senses and they get along just fine," I combated.

"But they still have *some* of their senses. What happens when you have none?"

I recoiled into my chair. How could someone be so wrong and still speak facts? As if I wasn't already confused by the universe, she made it seem like I knew less than I thought. This conversation trapped me in a vortex of knowing more than her, but still not enough.

I heard her sigh and noticed her gaze was back to the window. "Some people say death is another beginning."

It is.

"But they got it wrong."

No, they didn't.

"The truth is, when you die, you're no longer real. You're just a shell of your former self and eventually," she looked down at herself, waving her hand through her middle, "we'll all fade away."

The Clock turned red. Part of me was relieved to get out of this conversation, but another part of me didn't want it to end. I felt the need to convince her, but I didn't know how.

She dismissed herself, politely thanking me for the drink.

When she left, I realized the Clock ended the session because the spirit felt as though there was nothing left to discuss. In her mind, she understood. She wasn't at peace, though, she was dejected to her fate.

She brought up some good points. Souls and physical forms needed to work together to survive the Living World. However, the spirit was the consciousness of it all—the essence, the being, the identity—whatever you wanted to call it.

If she couldn't understand that, then I couldn't imagine her being a good candidate for taking my place as the Grim Reaper.

"Hi!"

Instantly, the departed soul greeted me as I arrived at their home. They had moved on in their sleep in the middle of the night, so the rest of the house was quiet. As far as I knew, no one had discovered the body yet.

"Hello," I replied.

"Are you here for me?"

"Yes."

She didn't seem bothered that she stood beside the Grim Reaper, nor did she seem to mind she was dead. Unless this was one of those situations where she thought it was a dream? Or maybe this was a rouse to butter me up to plead for her life.

"You're not who I expected," she observed, never once taking her eyes off me. There was a glint in her eyes, and I couldn't tell if it was from nerves or ... was it excitement?

"Who did you expect?" I played along.

"I thought I'd be surrounded by my loved ones who already left."

"Oh, I see."

"I've heard people say that when you die, the best seven seconds of your life flash before your eyes. You remember some of the best memories and people you've met during your time. I also heard that, when you're nearing the end, apparitions will appear to you. Old friends, grandparents, past pets ... they'd gather to help me cross to the other side."

"That all sounds wonderful," I stated. "But it's just me." For now.

She clicked her tongue, looking over her shoulder at her dead body lying in bed.

"Does that disappoint you?"

"A little." She hastily faced me again. "Not that I'm saying I don't want *you* here!"

I smirked. "I don't take offense." She wasn't pleading for her life, sobbing into my shoulder, or screaming in my face. Out of all the emotions, I didn't mind a little disappointment.

"When we get to the Spirit World, you'll be able to find your past loved ones."

Her smiled brightened. "So, they are still around?"

"Absolutely."

"So, can we go? Now?"

"Sure," I said, holding out my arm.

She stepped closer to me, wrapping her arm around mine, grinning up at me.

*

"This place is darker than I imagined," the spirit stated. She wandered around the Crossover Room, inspecting every nook and cranny. It's not like she'd find anything, though. We were surrounded by fake walls that mimicked an endless hallway.

"Care to sit?" I offered, already making her a cup of coffee. Excitedly, she bounced over to the table, sniffing her drink.

"How often can I get one of these?"

"Just here, I'm afraid."

She shrugged. "I'd rather enjoy something one more time knowing it's my last rather than never being able to enjoy it ever again."

"That's a smart way of thinking."

She nodded, putting her mug down on the table. That's when I noticed she had already drunk most of it. "A lot of people don't do certain things because they're afraid of the sad parts, but that's part of life," she explained to me. "You have to go through those sad times, disappointments, and miss something in order to keep being human. Otherwise, you can't properly balance your feelings and emotions. Being happy and safe all the time *sounds* ideal, but it can really mess you up. Take it from me. I know from experience. You need to balance the positive and negative or else you're a robot. Or else you wouldn't really be living."

I listened to her, stunned. She launched into the philosophical part of the conversation right away, but not because she needed guidance with anything. I didn't know where her words of wisdom came from, but it was refreshing to see she had already found her way in the Living World, and she carried that energy with her to the Afterlife.

The Spirit World needed more souls like that. They all got there eventually, but it was always nice to see a spirit already at peace. I knew right away that I'd have to ask her to come back for a group session.

"More?" she asked after downing the rest of her drink.

I refilled the cup, and she clapped her hands. She picked it up, and before drinking, said, "I couldn't have too much caffeine when I was alive because I'd give myself a panic attack. So, I was only able to have about three to four cups a day."

I nearly choked on my drink. Three or four sounded like a bit much, but I smiled and nodded along, anyway.

"Is there anything else here?" she changed the subject.

"You can find your loved ones, as I mentioned before," I answered. "You can also go back to the Living World and check in on those who are still alive. For the most part though, this is it."

"Can I go to my funeral?"

"If you'd like."

"I wonder who'll show up? I didn't have a lot of friends and I was the youngest of them. Not too many of us were left."

"I'm sure you'll have a good turnout."

She chuckled. "I hope so. I already planned the whole thing, so no one will have to do anything."

My eyes widened. "You planned your funeral?"

"Yeah."

"Were you expecting to move on soon?" I pressed. As far as I knew, she wasn't sick. She was older, but not elderly.

"Nope," she replied, shaking her head. "I don't even know how I died. I went to bed fine and woke up outside my body." She shrugged it off. "But anyway, I planned my funeral a long time ago. Saved up for it, too."

"Any particular reason why?"

"We all die at some point."

"True ..."

"And you never know when your time will come," she continued. "I wanted to be prepared. Grieving is a weighty feeling. Debilitating. Who wants to plan a funeral for a loved one when they're hurting so much? Who wants to scramble through their checkbooks to make sure they have enough to pay for the funeral home? The casket? The hole in the ground?" She shook her head, disgusted by the process. "No one should have to worry about that. Ever. That's why I knew when the time came for me to die, I'd already have that weight lifted from everyone else's shoulders."

"I'm impressed. Not everyone thinks to do that. Planning your own funeral is a heavy topic," I praised.

She raised her cup in thanks and continued drinking.

I had met souls before who were much older and had their funerals planned. Or their partner had already passed away, so they bought two plots in the cemetery instead of one. I had others worry about it after death because they had no money and neither did their family. Why the Living World created currency and attached it to everything, even the hard parts of living, was beyond me.

Then there were the spirits who didn't care if their loved one didn't have a funeral for them. They didn't want to put that pressure on their family and friends. Some desperately wanted a funeral and wanted to know who'd show up. Finally, some spirits wanted a funeral and didn't get one for various reasons. The disappointment was like heartbreak.

The blame was never on those in the Living World, though. Living was hard enough and planning a funeral was easily one of the most difficult things one has to go through when alive. No matter what happened, the spirits always understood why their loved ones did what they did. But it was never easy to accept at first.

"Hello?"

I snapped out of my thoughts when the soul waved a hand in front of my face.

She laughed. "Welcome back."

"I'm sorry ..." I said, embarrassed.

She flicked her wrist lazily. "I asked how you're doing."

"How ... *me*?"

She nodded, an amused grin on her face.

"Alright, I guess," I answered.

"You don't sound alright."

"I'm good." No one has ever asked me that before.

She hummed, sitting back in her chair. Her gaze lingered on me for another moment, but she let it go, turning her focus to the blue rose on the table. "That's pretty cool."

"Thank you."

"How come the rest of the place isn't decorated?"

I shrugged. "There's not much to decorate. No one is here for that long, anyway."

"What's that mean?" she inquired.

"The Crossover Room isn't a place where souls particularly hang out," I explained simply.

If reincarnation was explained to them, things would be a mess. Some spirits would be eager to go back to the Living World and try again, but others would want to relive the same life over.

In rare cases, it did work out that way. I didn't know why, but the bottom line was that they couldn't choose. They had no control over it and neither did I. If I explained it to them, they'd think I had more power than I actually have. It was similar to how most of them believed I caused death.

"Is this what you do all day?" she broke me out of my thoughts again.

"Why all the questions about me?" I skirted around the edge. "This session is supposed to be about you."

"What about me?"

"To help you move on."

"I did."

I raised a brow.

"I'm here, aren't I?" she asked.

"I meant mentally, emotionally. Not necessarily physically," I clarified.

She laughed. "Physically I'm like a wisp now!" she stood, stretching her arms out and twirling around as though she showed off a new dress she bought.

I couldn't help but grin.

"Do you think I can go through walls and stuff? Or is that just in the movies?" she tilted her empty mug to me, and I refilled it again, thankful caffeine didn't affect spirits.

"It takes practice and your soul will be solid when it needs to be," I said. "But is there anything else you'd like to discuss? About what to do next or where to go?"

She shook her head. "Do you like being the Grim Reaper?"

I froze, shaken by the question.

"It must be pretty cool, huh?" she continued, not realizing how uncomfortable the question made me. "You get to help so many people."

"I do," I replied. I'd be lying if I said I didn't enjoy that part, but that didn't make it any less exhausting.

"It must get lonely after a while, though. Watching everyone else move on while you have to be stuck in the Crossover Room. But if you enjoy it, then what's the harm? How did you become the Grim Reaper, anyway?"

I couldn't answer that.

"It must be so cool to know everything!"

I didn't know everything.

"When I was alive, I wasn't able to help people like I wanted. I'm sure I made a difference to some, but I didn't know how to go about helping people on a large scale. How can one individual touch the world? And to do so in a limited amount of time, and not knowing how much time that is, it's … it's tough."

I nodded.

"Sometimes you think you're doing the right thing, but then something will get in the way. Or people will say you can't do something, but you have to try, right?"

I kept nodding, listening intently.

"When people are alive, I believe we're meant to help people. It's such a privilege that you get to help from the other side."

A privilege? Is that what being the Grim Reaper was?

"It's a privilege to grow old," she continued. "Not everyone gets to do that. I didn't know if I'd be someone who'd get to grow old. That's why I did my best all the time. When you're young, people will tell you you're too inexperienced to do anything. They'll tell you that you don't understand and that it's hard to make a huge difference. One person can't do all that, can they? But I'm sure they can. All it takes is one person to start a chain reaction. One person to lead and others will follow."

She leaned forward, smiling excitedly at me. "If I were the Grim Reaper, I bet I could help so many other people in life and death!"

"You were enthusiastic …"

"How cool would that be?" the spirit leaned back in her chair again, smiling up at the ceiling as though she were picturing something wonderful in her mind.

The Clock turned red, and I wasn't sure why. Obviously, the soul was already at peace. She was so eager to be here, excited to go on her next adventure. Could that next adventure be becoming the Grim Reaper?

"… and I was desperate."

How desperate am I?

Sometimes spirits wouldn't click with each other, or they wouldn't talk at all. Those were the groups that caused me to question why I started group sessions in the first place.

The groups were meant to help me help the spirits further. I could only do so much and I knew, like in the Living World, the spirits could connect with one another and help each other out. We were a community no one knew existed. What else did we have if not each other?

Despite the sarcasm from the previous Grim Reaper, even they seemed to think the group sessions were a good idea. I had made a difference in the Afterlife, creating something no other Grim Reaper had done before. At least, not that anyone can remember.

In many ways, sure. I could see how being the Grim Reaper could be a curse. It was also a privilege. One I could use for good in order to help all the other spirits. Help guide them in moving forward and sharing their experiences with others to help further. We were all in this together, and I was the one who had the power to connect them all.

I was often nervous before group sessions, but not this one. I was eager to hear what these three spirits had to say to each other. Two women sat at the table with me and the man stood a few feet away. He still wanted to give his legs a good stretch.

The Clock shined green, illuminating the room as one of the ladies clapped and cheered for the man who danced in the middle of the room. The second woman cast me a confused glance, though I could see the amusement in her eyes. I shrugged as a weak response to her, not being able to hide my own content at how lively the other souls were.

The woman turned her back to me and faced the man. "What are you doing?" she asked, her tone curious.

"I'm dancing!" he exclaimed.

"But why?"

"I'm happy. I can move again."

"What do you mean?"

He finally stopped his dancing to answer. "I was paralyzed and in a wheelchair in the Living World. It's been so long since I've been able to use my legs. I still can't feel them, but they work. I forgot what it felt like to run around."

"Oh." It was all she could say.

"Is everything okay?" the other woman asked.

She replied with a shrug. "I thought we wouldn't be able to do a lot of the things our bodies could do once we died. I mean, we're spirits. We don't have all our senses anymore. We can't drive a car or go to work or go shopping. I know we can see friends and family, but what good is it if you can't communicate with them?"

"Do you know the saying when one door closes, another opens?" I asked, and she nodded. "It's a little like that. One life ended and you're starting a new journey. Nothing ever truly ends. The end means the beginning of something else. Everything is a cycle, and that includes life and death. You can't have one without the other."

She rolled her eyes. "You said that about our physical and spirit forms. You can't have one without the other, but we're all hollow no matter what form we're in. I can't tell if I'm my spirit or my body."

"Spirit, obviously," the man said, joining the conversation. He kicked one foot in the air again. "Otherwise, I wouldn't be able to do this again. My physical body had limitations, but my spirit doesn't."

"I agree," the other lady added. "We don't have all our senses anymore, but we still have the memories and lessons we learned. That's all stored somewhere in our spirit."

"No," she argued. "That's stored in our brains and our hearts and we don't have those anymore."

"Then how do you remember your previous life? According to your logic, you wouldn't remember anything about your time in the Living World. So, we wouldn't be having this conversation now."

Silence covered the room. I could see in her eyes that she wanted to have a smart remark in retaliation, but she couldn't think of anything. Instead, she crossed her arms and slouched down in her seat. Whether that was because of defeat or embarrassment, I wasn't sure.

"But we *are* hollow," she finally said, defiantly.

"In a way, yes," I said. We didn't have the organs a living being needed to function, nor did we have blood flowing through our veins—we didn't even have veins. No flesh to protect our bones, no skeletal outline. I did, but I supposed that was because I lived in the Afterlife while the other spirits were merely passing through. "Is that such a bad thing?"

I didn't understand why she got so caught up in the nothingness. I hoped to understand her feelings.

"It's weird," she answered simply. "We can't do anything in this form, so why do we have it? We can do so much in a physical body only for it to get ripped away. Why is it like that?"

Oh, she wanted to know the meaning behind life and death. Why the universe worked the way it did. Unfortunately, there wasn't an answer I could give.

"That's how things work." It was a bland statement, but true. "Life and death are a cycle and this is it. You can't explain why a caterpillar wraps itself in a cocoon and turns into a butterfly, can you? It's part of their cycle, something they do to survive. Spirits find a physical form to experience life in new ways, but it will always need to come back to its original form. A spirit."

"I couldn't use my legs before and now I can," the man joined the conversation. "It's almost as if, when we're in our spirit form, we sort of reset, if you will."

"The longer you live, the shorter your life," the other woman added.

The three of us stared at her. She was right, and it explained it so simply. I'd have to keep those words in my back pocket to explain it to other spirits.

However, the other woman shook her head in annoyance. "Then, why is it so gloomy here? If this is the original place, then why is it so dark? Why is there nothing here? The real world has everything."

Before I could answer, the other lady spoke up.

"It's not gloomy here. This is all we need."

Confused, the woman looked at her. "You mean we need nothing?"

She nodded. "Everything in the Living World is something we, in our physical forms, created. It's all materialistic things that we don't need. Instead of helping one another out, instead of forming together as a group, we delegate actions to others for money. We destroyed things to make our lives easier, like the environment. We forgot to be kind to each other. That's why—I think, anyway—the Afterlife is simple, because it's all we need."

I was relieved to see the other two souls drinking in her words. The Clock turned orange.

The man spoke up about his life. "All we need is each other." He told his story about his accident, about how his family made a new friend that day.

For a while, the three spirits swapped positive stories from their previous lives. It felt like I was no longer in the room, but I was okay with that. I sat back in my chair comfortably, listening to them gab and bond. The three spirits acted as though they were old friends. Maybe they had been a long, long time ago.

I wondered how each of these spirits would do as the next Grim Reaper. The man certainly understood not to take life for granted. One of the ladies still had a lot to learn, though her perspective of the universe was intriguing. The other woman seemed to have already figured it all out. Her confidence was contagious. She seemed the ideal candidate.

The Clock turned red after a few more minutes. The three of them exited, with only the enthusiastic woman waving goodbye to me.

The longer you live, the shorter your life. It was true for those in the Living World, but what about the Spirit World? How long were we here for before moving onto our next life?

I didn't even want to think about how long I've been the Grim Reaper. I wondered if I'd been utilizing my time in the Afterlife as well as I should have.

Is that why I hadn't moved on yet? I helped so many others move on that I forgot about myself.

PURPOSE

ONCE AGAIN, I HAD been left alone with my thoughts. I had seen many souls, brought so many spirits to the Afterlife without a break. I was tired, and I didn't normally feel that way. Despite the exhaustion, I couldn't imagine doing anything else. Yet, I had more lives to live.

Didn't I?

I must have lived my fair share of lives in the Living World before becoming the Grim Reaper. I don't remember those times from my existence. I was enthusiastic to be here, they had said. Did that mean I was interested in the Spirit World or was I happy I died?

I didn't remember.

Sometimes spirits would ask me questions about my time as the Grim Reaper. How did I get this job? Do I know all the answers? What am I keeping from them? Do I ever get lonely? Isn't the Grim Reaper supposed to have all the answers? Aren't I supposed to know how the universe works? Why do we live multiple lives?

I don't know. That's all I ever seem to say now.

Will I ever know?

It's difficult not knowing the answers when so much is expected from you. I knew countless spirits who looked at me with hope in their eyes. They'd look at me as though I was safe. In the Afterlife, I'm their only option. They don't get a choice in what happens next or who they encounter. However, once they begin to understand their death and find their peace, I'm the shoulder they can cry on. I'm the hand they can hold, the pillar they can lean against. I'm the vault they can confide in.

But what about me? Don't I have a pillar to lean on? Can I get anyone to lend an ear? Or was that selfish of me?

There's no rest for the Grim Reaper. The spirits need me. If I'm not there to pick them up from the Living World and help guide them in the Spirit World, what would happen to them? They'd be lost.

"I've been waiting for you."

I can't keep them waiting. They'll linger as an invisible shadow in the Living World forever.

"I'm not ready to let go!"

But what if I could give them just a little more time? No, time didn't exist in the way they interpreted it. It wouldn't matter.

"I don't have much of a choice, do I?"

No, I supposed not. None of us had a choice. The internal clock dictated how much time we had in the Living World. What we chose to do—or not do—in that time was completely up to us.

The Clock held most, if not all, the power in the Afterlife. We all had a piece of that clock in us when alive. Then, in the Spirit World, the Clock continued to tick for us. Why?

I don't know. After all this time, I still don't know.

"You must know something. Or else, why would you be in this position?"

But all I knew was the "how." Not the "why." I can explain to you the life cycle of the soul from the Spirit World to the Living World, then back to the Afterlife to repeat the process. Why were our spirits stuck in this cycle? Were we actually stuck, or did we only feel constrained? Did we have that feeling because, deep down, we knew we didn't use our time the best we could? We'll move on to a new life. We can try again. But by that time, we won't remember any of this happened. We'll fall back into old habits, but it'll be with different people. Different circumstances. Different reasons.

Is that such a bad thing? Or is it in our nature? Are our souls destined to constantly learn and grow, no matter what? No matter what we forget, are we fated to do better next time?

"Plants have no worries, why should I?"

Maybe I'm thinking too much.

"Why don't you know anything?"

Maybe I'm not.

"But when I forget ... what will I do then?"

You'll move on.

"Most of the time, you don't know when it'll be the last."

You'll move on without realizing it.

"I'm pretty sure I didn't cross the finish line before I died."

Is it possible to move on from an incomplete life?

"I died so others could live."

Is that the only reason you were placed in the Living World? What about you? Who was there to help you when you needed it? Why did your soul need to sacrifice its physical form for the sake of others?

"Why would I want to go back there?"

Life isn't meant to be easy.

"I can finally relax."

But only for a little while.

"When you die, you're no longer real."

No, our spirits make us real.

"I wanted to keep growing."

It's what makes us unique.

"I did a good thing ... didn't I?"

It's what makes us human.

I put my head in my hands, unable to stop the spirits' voices echoing in my mind. What was wrong with me?

"You were enthusiastic, and I was desperate."

Where had that enthusiasm gone? Am I desperate now? Is it time for me to move on?

*

I couldn't take it anymore. I stood, walking around the side of the table, to the other chair. I didn't want to rely on the previous Grim Reaper. I never needed guidance, but it wasn't so bad to ask for help once in a while, right? I sat down in the other chair before I could change my mind. Within seconds, the Grim Reaper appeared, sitting in my chair.

They looked around the room for a moment before settling their gaze on me. Their shoulders slumped in disappointment. "Oh, come on!"

"Hello again," I greeted.

"What do you want now?"

What *did* I want? The Clock knew I needed guidance and my instinct was to learn more from the previous Grim Reaper. However, I didn't know what I needed to ask.

We could discuss the meaning of life and death. I could ask them about the cycle, about why the universe works the way it does. But I didn't think that'd get me anywhere. Souls had asked me those questions before, and I wasn't able to answer them because they weren't supposed to know. If they had that knowledge, they'd change the way they live without realizing it.

Take those movies they make in the Living World, for example. If you knew your fate, how would you live? What would you do differently? Most people would change the way they live to either delay their fate or attempt to change it. Having that knowledge wouldn't actually help them, it would only make fate work faster. They'd cause their fate by trying to avoid it.

A bony hand waved in front of my face and I focused on the Grim Reaper leaning over the table. They glared at me as they sat down again.

"What did you want?"

"You remember our previous conversation?" I asked.

"Yes."

"Interesting."

"What?"

"I thought you wouldn't remember, thinking it was all a dream."

"When I'm awake, yes," they replied. "I was super groggy and felt like I didn't get any sleep at all, but now that I'm here as the Grim Reaper, I remember. You know, I have a big meeting at work tomorrow and I'm going to be exhausted for it because of you."

"My apologies," I said sincerely.

"Whatever." They rolled their eyes. "Just tell me what you need."

Need. What did I need?

"I want to get back home."

Home. The Afterlife wasn't their home anymore. It didn't belong to them, it belonged to me.

"If you could bring one thing from the Living World over to the Afterlife, what would it be?" I asked.

The Grim Reaper narrowed their eyes. "... What?"

I didn't know why I asked that, either, but I rolled with it. "You know that hypothetical question souls ask each other in their physical forms? If you were stuck on an island?"

"Yeah, I know of it," they said, annoyed. "What does that have to do with anything here?"

"Pretend the Afterlife is an island. You can only bring one thing here from your previous time in the Living World. What would you bring?"

They sat taller, folding their hands on the table. "You brought me back here to ask me a hypothetical question?"

I pressed my lips together, unresponsive. They were annoyed, that much was clear, but I wanted an answer, nonetheless. Why? I wasn't sure yet.

"You know we can't carry anything over, so why bother?" they pressed.

"Hypothetical," I reminded.

They groaned, leaning back. Tilting their chin upward in thought, the room fell into silence. I didn't expect them to think so deeply about the question, but I waited patiently for their response.

It was then I realized I didn't have an answer myself. What was once important to me from previous lives that I no longer remembered?

I thought about the people I might have loved in previous lives. Parents, grandparents, siblings, close friends ... would I dare cut any of their time short just so I could be with them in the Spirit World?

Then I thought about the soul who said goodbye to everything, including a puzzle book. Did I have any objects of importance to me in from my previous lives? What objects would be worth remembering? Worth holding onto?

There was the spirit who mentioned bringing a photo album. It'd be easy to remember the fond memories I made with the faces of people I once loved. Or would that be torture to remember what I used to have?

"I wouldn't bring anything," the Grim Reaper said matter-of-fact.

"Nothing?" I stiffened in my seat.

"Nothing."

"Why?"

"Why would I bring anything in the first place?"

"Wouldn't you want to remember anything?"

They sighed. "Where is this coming from? Is it because you can't remember anything about your previous lives?"

I opened my mouth, but they didn't let me speak.

"I know many people would answer they'd bring something to help them get off the island. Is that what you're fishing for? You want me to give you a hint of how to get out of the Afterlife? You want off the island?"

"That's not it at all," I replied, offended. Although, I wondered, deep down, if that's what I wanted.

"I already told you what you need to do."

Sure, I knew what I *needed* to do, but is that what I wanted?

"But why nothing? If you had the opportunity to bring something, would you really leave everything behind?" I pressed.

"I'm going to forget all about it anyway, so why bother?"

"You only know that because you were the Grim Reaper once. If you don't know you'd forget about it, would you still not bring anything with you?"

They rolled their eyes again, but the Clock was still green. I could argue about this for as long as it takes.

"Forget the island," they said, "what about a fire?"

I shook my head. "I don't understand." They still didn't answer my question.

"There's another hypothetical scenario people ask. If your house burned down and you had enough time to save one item, what would it be?"

I shrugged. I didn't know what I'd have in my house in the first place. It'd been so long since I had a roof over my head. Yet, I had a feeling I knew what they meant.

On an island, some people would bring items with them that would help them relax. They'd view it as a break because, for most people, a tropical island is the ideal vacation spot. However, none of them consider the weather when a storm hits. They don't consider the loneliness that would slowly take residence in their mind.

Others would bring something on the island to help them get home. It's a temporary situation for them.

You could tell a lot about a person based on their answer.

The first answer represented giving up. Not in a negative way, but it had multiple meanings. They might not trust themselves to get out of that situation, they don't believe in themselves, or they don't want to try at all. So, they bring items to help them relax. Or maybe they genuinely live a tough life and ache for a break. They're tired.

The second answer represented tenacity. They still have much to live for, have loved ones back home they'll miss. They have responsibilities to get back to.

One could argue the first answer was something the person *wanted* to do, while the second answer was something the person *needed* to do. There were no wrong answers, and I believed a person's answer would change from time to time depending on their current situation.

Life isn't always positive. We all have a mix of memories filled with happiness, sadness, anger, confusion, disappointment, regret, and everything in between. One day, being stuck on an island must sound lovely. Another day, it must sound scary. Our wants and needs fluctuate. That's just human nature.

Now what if your house burned down and you could only salvage one item? That was an entirely different situation. You didn't get a choice of escape or not. There was no hope of making it back to the home you once knew. You'd have to start over from scratch.

Yet, people would answer one of two ways.

First, there was the practical answer. They'd rush into their home and grab their important documents or emergency cash. They'd grab whatever they could to help them start over.

Or there was the less practical answer, but still equally important. They'd make sure their pet got out alive. They'd take that family heirloom from a past loved one. They'd grab that photo album.

What can't you give up? What do you need to do versus what you want?

Both questions were weird in my opinion. What were the odds of getting stuck on an island? The fire was something that could—and did—happen to many people every day. They didn't get a choice or a break. Why was the fire such a real possibility and the island was a fun, quirky scenario?

It all had to do with fate. You can prepare all you want, but in the end, in the heat of the moment, you wouldn't actually do what you said you would. Your fight or flight would kick in. Your brain would freeze in shock. We'd all like to imagine we'd brave that burning building and be the hero, but the truth was, many of us would be too afraid to do anything in the moment.

Similar to the island, your answer to the fire scenario would also change depending on the day, depending on what's going on in your life. We have many important things and people for us in the Living World. How can you choose just one?

Need versus want.

"Let me put it this way for you," the Grim Reaper cut through the silence. I snapped out of my own head to pay attention to them. They smirked at me. "For me, the Afterlife is an island. For you, the Afterlife is the fire."

My voice caught in my throat. Why did I get the feeling they were making fun of me?

Their grin grew. "The difference is I can get off this island, but you're caught in the fire. Every life I live is an island on its own, which is why I wouldn't bring anything with me. I know the next island will have its ups and downs, it'll have good people and bad, but it's nothing I can't handle. But you? Your previous life burned down and now you're stuck in the Afterlife because you decided to stay put."

"I didn't decide anything," I countered. "You made me stay here when you made me take your place because ..."

"You were eager," they agreed. "Is that a good enough reason for me to choose you? Maybe, maybe not. For a while, the Afterlife was my fire, and I chose to start over. Do you know what I took with me from my previous life? What I saved from that fire?"

I shook my head.

"Guess. It's nothing tangible."

I couldn't think of an answer.

"Determination. Fierceness. Hope," they stated. "When something happens to you, you can either let it happen or do something about it. I'm not the type to sit around and see what happens. If I'm stuck on an island, I'll find a way off that island. If I'm caught in a fire, I'll build sturdier walls."

It was admirable, I had to admit. Even though I didn't care about their attitude most of the time, they had a point. When something happens to you that you don't like, only you have the power to change it. Only you can live your life however you want.

Want.

"I did what I needed to do to get out of this place because I had the will to do so. Can you say the same thing about yourself?"

Need.

What did I want? What did I need? Was one more important than the other? Which was it?

Ultimately, the goal was to get out of the Afterlife. For me to move on and begin my next life in the Living World, destined to repeat that cycle for eternity like everyone else who inhabited this universe.

"Tell me about some of the recent souls you've talked to," the Grim Reaper suggested. "Since I'm here, I'll help you out a little." Their tone wasn't sincere. Instead, it was filled with snark, as if they were doing me a favor.

I ignored their attitude, though. "There are a few spirits who come to mind."

They smiled. "Good, so you've been thinking about it."

I guess I had been thinking about it, not that I realized it.

I spoke of the gardener first, explaining why I believe they'd be a good fit. "Overall, I appreciate their outlook on life and how they compared humans to plants. They're all living beings."

"No, not good enough," the Grim Reaper hissed.

"Why not?" I asked, shocked.

"If all they're going to do is talk about plants and gardening, how are any of the spirits going to know to move on?"

I supposed they had a point, but I thought it was endearing, nonetheless. The gardener was able to connect something so real from the Living World into everyone else's life. They were right in the sense that we did have a lot to learn from plants. We needed to care for them just as we needed to care for ourselves and others. I didn't see anything wrong with that. It was a new perspective on life, yet something everyone could relate to even if they didn't garden.

Then again, I supposed talking about plants all the time would get old and possibly confusing. After all, we weren't actually plants.

"Tell me about someone else," they prompted grumpily.

I thought for a moment. "There was this elderly woman. She was already at peace when I picked her up. She was waiting for me."

"So?"

I shrugged.

"Not good enough."

"Why?" I groaned.

"Of course, older people are going to be ready to move on from their time in the Living World. They're old, they've lived their lives. That doesn't mean they were good at living it, and that certainly doesn't mean they'd make a good Grim Reaper."

I nodded, taken aback at the harshness of their tone. I didn't necessarily agree with them, though. The woman reminisced about the time she spent with her husband and how fond she was of the rain. She was another who saw the good in things most people didn't care for. The rain helped us to slow down and observe what's around us. It helped us realize that, in order to live, we needed good and bad. That balance allowed us to make mistakes and learn from them.

I didn't bother explaining that, though, knowing the Grim Reaper wouldn't want to hear it. I was confused why they cared so much when I was the one who spoke to these souls, not them.

"Anyone else?" they grunted.

"There was a young—"

"A kid?"

I shifted my weight in my chair. "Yes. What's the matter now?"

"Way too young."

I glared at them. "There's no such thing. You, of all spirits, should know time doesn't exist. There's no correct age to arrive at the Afterlife."

"But you can't have a kid in charge of the Spirit World," they countered. "A kid has no living experience."

"They spent time in the Living World. I would call that experience." Out of most of the souls I spoke to, children seemed to have the best grasp on life *because* they were so young. They didn't spend too much time in the Living World, no, but that meant they didn't have a chance to get corrupted by material things or temptations. They only knew innocence and kindness.

"Who else?"

"Why do you care?" I snapped. "Isn't this supposed to be my choice?"

The Grim Reaper laughed. "You think you have a choice? This is all about fate. When I said you needed to find someone to take your place, I didn't mean for you to dissect each spirit and their morals. The next Grim Reaper will show themselves in due time, and when you come across them, you'll know exactly who they are."

I froze. I did know who they were.

"Ultimately, you need to do this for yourself. Be a little selfish, you've earned that much," they stated.

What did being selfish even mean to me? I was meant to help spirits. That was my purpose, wasn't it? No, that was the Grim Reaper's purpose. Who was I before this? And the time before that? And who am I meant to be when I'm no longer the Grim Reaper?

"So, it was my destiny to be the Grim Reaper?" I questioned.

They shrugged. "Fate probably had something to do with it. When I saw you, I just knew."

"Because you thought I'd do a good job? Because I was enthusiastic?"

"Because I was desperate. I did what I needed to do for me. I didn't care if you did a good job or not."

I narrowed my eyes. Here they were, making a big fuss over my choices. Hypocrite.

"And you need to get out of here, too. Isn't that what you want?"

I didn't know. Did I *need* to move on from being the Grim Reaper? Or did I *want* to move from being the Grim Reaper? Were both answers the same?

When I didn't answer, the Grim Reaper waved their hands around. "Why else would you have called me here again?"

Why did I call them again? Their guidance has been anything but helpful.

"I assumed you needed my help to move on, right?"

Although, they shed some interesting insights for me. I realized I didn't need their help at all, nor did I want it. So, why did I call them back here?

As the Grim Reaper, I needed to help souls move on from one life to the next. Was that because that was the Grim Reaper's job? But I also wanted to help spirits move on from one life to the next. Was that because that's all I knew?

No matter the reasons, my wants and needs were the same. They were balanced on a scale, because how else are you supposed to live? The only way to move forward is to do what you need, but you need to sprinkle in what you want or else you'll never be happy. I did what I needed to, but, over time, I realized I wanted to keep doing it.

I thought about the soul who had stuck out to me all this time. She was eager to be here, just as I was once upon a time. She was at peace with her death, and she already knew the differences between the Living World and the Spirit World. She could see the differences and similarities between life and death.

In reality, all we needed was each other. Someone to lean on, talk to, and each other's company. The Afterlife was a place for spirits to connect and reconnect with one another. I enjoyed bringing spirits closer together, that's why I started the group sessions, and they worked.

Have I brought these spirits as far as they can go? Could this soul improve the Afterlife beyond what I could do for it?

"You're thinking of someone else, aren't you?"

I looked up, seeing the Grim Reaper smiling at me. For a moment, I forget they were here. I nodded but didn't speak. Was it the right choice?

"You were enthusiastic, and I was desperate."

"Who is it?" they asked.

I shook my head.

They frowned. "What's the matter?"

"They're not the right fit, either," I murmured.

"You looked awfully sure."

You don't know anything about me.

"Come on, who is it?"

"I thought I was desperate, but I'm not," I stated bluntly.

"Huh?" they raised a brow.

I leaned forward in my chair. "You told me you wouldn't bring anything with you if you were deserted on an island. What about that fire?"

"Still nothing," they chuckled.

"Why?"

"I wouldn't need anything."

"Yes, you would."

The Grim Reaper sneered at me as though I had insulted them. "Then tell me. What would I need?"

"A soul."

They threw their head back and bellowed, their laughter echoing the Crossover Room. "I have a soul. We're all spirits."

"Not *your* soul," I clarified. They stopped laughing, now confused.

So, I explained. "It doesn't matter if you're stuck on an island or need to start completely over. It also doesn't matter if you're passing through the Afterlife or if you're here to stay for a while. In order to move on, you'd bring a soul. Not because you want to, but because you need to. You'd need to replace your soul with someone else's. That's exactly what you did. You traded my soul for yours so you could move, and I'd be stuck here."

They didn't respond. I couldn't read their expression now. Were they impressed? Did they feel guilty? Indifferent?

"But I'm not stuck here," I declared. "I never thought I was until I met you. Sure, I sometimes wondered what being alive again felt like, but I never thought about finding a way to be alive again until you presented the idea to me. I don't think I saw it before because I never thought about leaving the Afterlife. I accepted my fate, my role as the Grim Reaper. I'm pretty good at it, too, if I say so myself."

I didn't let them speak. "Is it tiring? Yes. There are many souls I feel like I could have helped more. Is it thankless? Sometimes. More often than not, I'm depicted as the bad guy. Is it frustrating? Absolutely. No matter how many times I explain myself, I'm always viewed as death. No matter how I try to help, I can't always get through to a spirit. Sometimes I don't even know if I can help." I grinned. "But is it fulfilling? Yes, it is. I can't count the number of spirits who have left the Crossover Room with a smile on their face. It's rewarding. My aim is to connect souls together, and that's exactly what I've accomplished so far. I think some souls have more friends here in the Spirit World than they did when they were alive. There are so many ups and downs about having this task, but it's a positive experience if you want to look at it that way. And I do look at it that way. Not every spirit is created equal and some are tougher than others, but there are also many spirits who teach me in return. Because, like them, I still have so much to learn about the universe and about living, even though I don't have the same luxury as being in the Living World like they do."

I stood, looking down upon the previous Grim Reaper, as they stared back up at me with arms folded, slouched in their chair. "I know I've made a difference for all these spirits, even if they won't remember it when they enter their next life. But if I can have a positive impact, even if just for a short while, I think it's worth it. If I can make their time easier being here, then it's worth it. Being the Grim Reaper is worth it.

"The spirits who I thought would be a good fit to be the next Grim Reaper would do an amazing job, but I'm not willing to trade their soul for mine. Those spirits are needed in the Living World, just as I'm needed in the Afterlife. I *want* to continue being the Grim Reaper and the next Grim Reaper after that. I *need* to. I want to be the Grim Reaper as much as I need it. I can't imagine doing anything else. And that's my selfish answer."

The Clock turned orange at my last statement. The Grim Reaper noticed and snickered under their breath. They stood, smiling at me. It wasn't condescending, either. It was a genuine smile.

"Congratulations," they said, holding out their hand to me.

With caution, I shook their hand.

"You've realized your soul's purpose. The majority of us are still figuring that out for ourselves. I'd say I'm jealous, but … I'm know one of these lives will show me my purpose."

Relieved at the kind words, I felt my shoulders relax. "It's a journey to be alive."

The Clock turned red.

The previous Grim Reaper dipped their head politely. "I'll see you on the other side," they said, their voice and self fading away to nothing.

*

I lingered where I stood for a long time once I was alone again. Many thoughts and feelings swirled through my head. Although, I couldn't tell you what I thought about. Words didn't form well as I thought about the endless conversations I've had with countless souls, with the previous Grim Reaper, and finally, the conversations I've had with myself.

Life wasn't easy, but neither was death. They were so different and so much the same. More than I realized.

There were many times I felt sad for the spirits I met. Many times I'd feel lonely, even though I was surrounded by so many souls. Spirits were meant to be there for one another, but we didn't interact as we did in the Living World.

The souls might be confused, depressed, or scared, but the more they let their feelings out—to me or other spirits—they'd lighten up. They'd remember the good times and the bad, talk about their loved ones—ones who have already moved on and who they left behind. Their growth was amazing to watch. What a privilege it was to touch so many lives.

I walked over to the window and stared through the frame that so many spirits looked through. I didn't imagine my destiny turning out this way. Then again, no one knows their fate until they're faced with it. The reason our fate is so different from someone else's is because we all play a vital role in the universe.

The void through the window changed, and I finally saw what so many spirits saw. It brought a tear to my eye and a smile to my face.

After a moment, I peeled my gaze away from the window and walked to the other side of the table. I sat down in the Grim Reaper's chair. My chair.

Instantly, the Clock turned yellow. With this new sense of clarity, I was enthusiastic once more, eager to help another soul in a Crossover session.

Being the Grim Reaper was who I was meant to be. Your purpose may take a long time to find and sometimes it's the least expected road. It's a confusing path and might not feel natural at first. But being who you are—who you're meant to be—is the most beautiful feeling in the universe.

Acknowledgements

Many people behind the scenes made this book possible.

First, thank you to all who have bought and read Apparitions Anonymous. If it weren't for those who bought it, read it, and reviewed it, I'd probably think people wouldn't care about a sequel. That said, thank you to all the readers of this book. I hope something resonated with you, and despite the subject, I hope you enjoyed the ride. I appreciate your choosing to spend time with my work.

Second, my family has always supported my creative writing journey. Mom, Dad, Lisa, Kris, Jackie, and Kat are my biggest fans, and I couldn't be more thankful.

I also want to thank my old writing group. Even though it died with Covid, I still have its general feedback and words of wisdom in the back of my head whenever I write. So, thank you to Morgan, Casey, and Marina. (Lin, too, in spirit since you were never part of the writing group, but I appreciate you anyway!)

Thank you to Ari, as always. She has always been a huge supporter of my work in more ways than one. I'm so proud to walk the author's path with her, and she always inspires me to keep going.

To my Caffeinated Club members: Mom, Kris, Jackie, and Rick—thank you! Without your support on Ko-fi, this book would have taken longer to get out into the world.

Finally, I'm giving myself a pat on the back. Some of these stories were tough to get through, and lots of things happened during my life while Happily Ever Afterlife was a work in progress. I'm proud of myself for persevering and sticking to my goals, even when it was tough to do so.

Thank you again for reading Happily Ever Afterlife. This book was never supposed to exist, but here we are. After giving the Grim Reaper an existential crisis in the first book, I thought it was only fair to give them closure. I'm happy to have written this next set of stories, though. In a difficult and fast-paced world, I hope this batch of shorts allows you to sit back and view life a little differently. Take time for self-care, call a friend you haven't spoken to in a while, and give your family members a hug.

Thanks again, and please take care of yourself.

ABOUT THE AUTHOR

Rachel Poli is a cozy fiction author, dipping her toes in cozy mystery, cozy fantasy, and the metaphysical. She writes short stories, novels, and the occasional flash fiction piece.

Her work explores the obscurities of life through themes of love, loss, and mental health. These stories unleash genuine emotion that will leave you with deep thoughts.

In her spare time, she's usually organizing something or playing video games with a coffee in hand. She lives in New England with her zoo.

Connect with Rachel
Website: RachelPoliAuthor.com
Join the Caffeinated Club: Ko-fi.com/RachelPoli
Instagram: @RachelP_Reads

Books by Rachel Poli

The Grim Reaper Files

Apparitions Anonymous
Happily Ever Afterlife

Flash Fiction

Sunday Morning

www.ingramcontent.com/pod-product-compliance
Lightning Source LLC
Chambersburg PA
CBHW071127100726
47908CB00008B/2520